# VAMPIRE ASSASSIN
## LEAGUE

# BARBARIAN

INCLUDES:
**A FOREVER MATE**
**EXIST**

## Jackie Ivie

# A FOREVER MATE

Jackie Ivie

# CHAPTER ONE

*Paris*

One small word, in tiny font appeared on his monitor. It sent an eerie yellow glow into his cavernous chamber. Sebastian watched the word flicker on his monitor for a few moments before he typed his answer.

'I detest Paris.'

The answer was immediate. In bolder font.

*You detest most things.*

'You know the reason.'

*Inconsequential. Your assignment is in Paris.*

'Give it to someone else.'

*You're closest.*

'I'm in Bruges.'

*Grab a cell.*

The screen went dark. The chamber about him lost its lone source of illumination as the little blue connection light faded. Sebastian reached for the eight-pack of slim-phones in his back pocket. He pulled one out. He didn't like phones, either, but it was now his fault.

He'd listed his location.

On the World Wide Web.

Where it could be traced.

He'd probably have to move to the caverns beneath Castle Venderlyn now. He pondered that while he waited. It wasn't much of an issue. All his homes were pretty much the same, richly-furnished. Private. Quiet. Dark. They were all deep in the ground beneath ancient castles that doubled as sometime-inns. That disguised his electrical usage. And any errant smoke... if he made a fire in a fireplace.

*Hmm.* He couldn't recall the last time he'd made a fire. No need for the light, the heat, or the ambiance. The phone in his palm vibrated. He slid the receiver open and put it to an ear.

"Sebastian... Cole."

His name came with authority and power, as if intoning a lengthy sentence. It also carried a hint of amusement. He was dealing with the head of the Vampire Assassin League. One of Akron's attributes was a powerful voice. The speaker on Sebastian's cell phone crackled with bass tones. Sebastian smirked before mimicking the greeting. Exactly.

"Akron... Profit."

"You have an assignment. In Paris."

"Not interested."

"It involves a politician."

Sebastian hesitated, momentarily paused. He detested Paris, but he really hated politicians. "Have someone else do it."

"Actually... I should clarify some more. The assignment actually entails a bit of sex and sleaze along with the politics."

"So?"

"I'm trying to pique your interest."

"You failed."

Sebastian clicked the lid shut on his credit-card sized phone. His entire back pocket jolted with the reaction as more than one cell phone rang. He reached back and pulled the pack out, slid out another. Opened it. Put it to his ear.

"Don't hang up on me again, Sebastian. You won't enjoy the consequences."

Sebastian considered his options. None of them were acceptable. He'd discovered that back in the seventeenth century when he'd physically fought Akron.

He'd lost.

"Why me?" he asked finally.

"Like I said... you're closest."

"There are eight associates in France."

"Probably more."

"And I'm closest?"

Akron chuckled. "I really do like you, Sebastian. You're quick. Argumentative. Confident. And entirely too stuck in your ways. This is your hit. Trust me."

"Negative."

"Whoa. I can't believe my ears, Sir. He's telling you no. You."

That sounded like Nigel, the youngest assassin, and the most annoying. That wasn't amusing. Sebastian hadn't known Nigel was listening in. There was a bit of silence before Akron answered.

"I believe I'm getting that message as well, Nigel. Thank you for bringing it up."

"What did he do?" Sebastian asked.

"Who?"

"Your politician."

"Oh. Him. He hired us."

"A politician hired us? Why? He can't win an election without bumping off his opponent?"

"Nothing like that. It's more in the sex and sleaze arena. You see... our client recently wed a beautiful young woman. Let me place the emphasis on young. And beautiful. She's sexy. Exotic. She barely speaks his language. I believe she is what is called a 'trophy wife' in his circle."

"Sounds like the sex part is covered."

"And she's insatiable."

"Lucky man."

"Oh. No. You misunderstand. Our man is – to put it delicately – mature. He is not keeping his wife satisfied. And then he exacerbated the situation by hiring several young, fit, male bodyguards. Is this making sense to you, yet?"

"Let me guess. These bodyguards are doing a bit too much close body work with the wife, nobody signed a pre-nup, and our man likes his money and his career. So, who is the hit? The wife?"

"Oh. No. Our politician adores her. He almost wishes he hadn't hired a private investigator and learned the extent of his wife's nymphomania."

"Right. Sounds like a case of true love. So... the hit is on the so-called bodyguards? How many are we talking?"

"You're getting ahead of me, Sebastian. You need to look a little deeper. Politicians hide from bad publicity. He actually hired the P.I. so he could ascertain what kind of damage might come out if he does run for office."

"Well, of course. Politicians are usually thinking ahead. So. It's the wife *and* the bodyguards, then? Does he own a small private plane? It can be quick. Clean. Untraceable. Hell, even Nigel could handle it."

"What? Now, hang on a minute! Just because I'm not as big and bad as some of you guys does not make me incompetent. Sir. Let me handle it. Please? I really need the experience."

"Nigel. Has it ever occurred to you that certain things might be said in your hearing to get a certain reaction?"

"All the time, Sir."

"Then, perhaps you could consider ignoring Cole's words this time?"

"What reaction would the big-bad, barbarian, Sebastian Cole, be looking for?"

"Oh... I would hazard a guess that he's searching for something that might get him off the hook on this assignment. And look there. You jumped right onto the bait."

"But I could handle this hit. You should let me."

"I already said it. This is Sebastian's hit. Trust me. We're out of time. Sebastian. You still there?"

"Yes."

"Grab another phone."

The line went dead. Sebastian put the phone on the table next to his laptop. He'd crush it later. The VAL always used disposable cell phones and non-traceable numbers. He almost had the next phone opened before it vibrated.

"Sebastian? Good. Apologies. I don't usually waste so much time and words. Your hit is actually the private investigator. Harold Bracket. He wins the sleaze prize this go-around. Apparently, he decided to try his hand at blackmail. And if our politician doesn't cough up the funds, the file on the wife is going public. That is something our client refuses to allow. I charged him triple what the P.I. was asking, because we're doing a clean-up of all files afterwards. He said it's worth it."

"Money doesn't matter to me."

"I know. Oh. And Sebastian?"

"Yes?"

"Stay out of the catacombs."

He slapped the lid shut and flung the phone. The crunch as it shattered against a wall was loud. But it wasn't satisfying.

# CHAPTER TWO

Harold Bracket appeared to be an excellent private investigator. He was a hair under average height... perhaps five foot seven. He had a bald spot at the crown of his head that he covered over with a 'comb-over' effect. He could be extremely fit, but he disguised it beneath nondescript dungarees that needed washing, a dark-toned, button-up shirt, and a faded denim jacket. He'd been hard to locate in the dark streets and alleys he'd decided to inhabit this evening.

If his killer was afoot, Harold would be difficult to track as well.

Sebastian tilted his head to one side as he peered down into the tenth alley in as many minutes. He was atop the railing of a fire escape this time. Next to the brick wall of some four story tenement. Just below the roof eave, using it for shadow. Harold and his prey were moving rapidly now. That was interesting. The P.I. was obviously on a case, continually stalking a jittery young man who appeared to be under the influence of some psychedelic drug. It was actually easier to track the druggie and then back-track to Harold's location.

The private investigator also seemed to have a sixth-sense about his environment. More than once he'd appeared to check about surreptitiously, as if aware he was under scrutiny, but unable to verify. He had a nasty habit of chain-smoking, however. And an equally nasty cough. He was probably flirting with some cardio-pulmonary disease if he wasn't already suffering it. That might explain his foray into blackmail. He might be looking to retire... before the cancer killed him.

*Hmm.* Looked like he was handling a mercy killing, not just a hit. That should alleviate some of the gloom that surrounded him.

It didn't.

Out here, it was hard to think of Paris as the city of light. Or the capital of love. Or a city of life. Verve. Imagination. No. To him, Paris was dark. Distasteful. Ugly. And the longer he lingered, the more the bitterness grew. Something perverse made it happen, too. He could have taken out Harold any number of times, but something made this delay part of his penance.

To Sebastian, Paris was a reminder of failure.

He dropped soundlessly to the railing below him, and then the one beneath that, hovering at the second floor fire escape. Just above Harold's head. The guy was coughing again, shoving his face beneath the right lapel of his jacket, apparently trying to keep it quiet. Somewhere in the street he watched, Harold's junkie was buying a fix. Maybe even shooting it up. Sebastian didn't look. He didn't care. He'd finished wasting time.

He dropped into the spot before Harold. The guy looked up, and then stumbled back, reacting instantly to the threat. He had a wicked-looking blade in one hand, too. Sebastian grinned.

"Good eve, Harold," he said.

"Who the hell are you?"

He'd been off a bit on Harold's height. The fellow was diminutive. Or Sebastian's six foot, six inch size was larger than it used to be. He looked down at the fellow, and his smile broadened. This time he let his canines grow. He watched Harold's eyes grow larger. Round. Harold worried needlessly. Sebastian wasn't fond of nicotine.

"I believe tonight... you can call me... Reaper," Sebastian said. And then he smacked Harold right in the chest.

The P.I. snapped back several feet, both hands clutching at his chest as if that could restart his heart. He made gulping noises, while his mouth worked to suck at air. His eyes were still wide as he sank to the ground at their feet, but he wasn't seeing anything. He was dead before he hit the mud. Face first. If all went well, the medical unit would suspect a heart attack and fail to check for postmortem bruising under the skin.

Sebastian didn't truly care. It was over. He headed now toward the one place Akron had told him not to. The underground city of the dead. Officially the Ossuary of Paris, but always called the catacombs.

Because his penance included this, as well.

It took him awhile to reach the right area. It wasn't due to incompetence, or loss of direction. His approach slowed as he neared the arrangement of human bones that decorated the walls of the catacomb. It was as if his feet were mired in quicksand, bogging him down. Making each movement more difficult. More poignant. Blacker. The tunnels hadn't been crafted for a man of his size, either. He'd stooped more than once, and even that dragged at him.

And then he was there.

At the place where the bones from the Church of Saint Nicolas des Champs had been placed.

The place that held *her*.

His Isabelle. His wife.

Sebastian put his head back and howled, the sound echoing and re-echoing back to him. It didn't matter. The catacombs were empty this time of night. The tunnels leading to this section had all been black. Eerie. They didn't have much light in this area but that didn't hamper him. He found the marker: *"OSSEMENTS DE LANCIEN CIMETIERE ST NICHOLAS DES CHAMPS DEPOSES DE 1843... TRANSFERES DANS LES CATACOMBES..."*

Sebastian went to his knee before it.

This plaque was all he had to show that Isabelle's remains had been ripped from her grave, piled onto a cart for transportation, and then dumped into a tunnel that held millions of bones. Nobody had kept track of names. Dates. Grave markers. Sebastian faced a sea of bones. He didn't even know which ones were hers.

This was the reason he hated politicians. They were the ones allowing this desecration, this transfer, the creation of this macabre display. They'd needed the ground for the living. The dead could simply move.

Sebastian bent his head down, his view taking in the scuffle of footprints on the dirt beneath his knee. The area had seen a lot of foot traffic recently. He didn't know why anyone bothered. Images were available in graphic detail on any internet search. And yet, they'd made the bones of his beloved nothing more than a tourist attraction.

*Merde*. He really detested Paris.

If he had sensation, he'd probably feel grief, experience pain... maybe even rage. But all that was gone. Just like his Isabelle. She'd been lost the moment he left her side. Isabelle had been stricken by the plague. Nobody could help. Nobody would even approach. So Sebastian had washed her body down with water, wrapped her in sumptuous blankets, and gone on a quest.

Sebastian was a rare creature. He hadn't been saved from death by a vampire bite. He'd been healthy, strong, and desperate. He'd actively pursued tales and sightings of the monstrous creatures. And one night, Akron had appeared. Sebastian had begged and pleaded and been granted his wish. He needed immortality. For her.

But it had taken time. He'd been too late.

And this was the result.

He stood, and bent to dust his knee. He'd picked up several sharp shards on his leather trousers. As if someone had broken something glass-like. They pricked his fingers as he brushed. It stung slightly. Sebastian turned his hand over and watched as the tiny cuts closed up and disappeared.

*Odd.*

For a moment there, he'd almost felt... something. Sebastian lifted his head and looked down one tunnel and then the other direction. Nothing but rows of arranged bones, dimness that led to more of the same, silence that had a weight to it. He hadn't noticed it before, but the temperature was cooler down here. Almost chilly. It wasn't bothersome. It was simply an observation. Sebastian shook his head. He was imagining. Vampires didn't feel anything. Never had. Never would.

He took a deep breath. Held it for long enough it pained. Released it. He might as well leave. He'd done what he came to do. Harold Bracket was dead. The League was at work erasing files and eliminating evidence at his office and his home. And he'd paid his respects to his one true love. His life.

His heart thumped heavily at the thought. And then it did it again.

And again.

On the third beat Sebastian's mouth went wide, stretching his jaw. His eyes followed. His limbs went weak next. His legs wobbled. And then he dropped onto both knees. His sword landed somewhere beside him. He watched it without really seeing it.

Was it possible?

He was breathing?

Oh. This was bad. This only happened if a vampire found their one true mate. The one creature designated throughout time for them. He couldn't have a mate. He'd already had one. He'd loved Isabelle too deeply. She owned his heart. She always would. Gooseflesh raced along his skin next, lifting bumps. Sebastian tried to stop the shivers. He tightened every muscle. Held his chest from inhaling. Willed his heart to cease beating. Tried to force the reanimation to cease.

Nothing worked.

All that happened was a repetitive dull pounding as his heart hammered away in his chest, while his muscles grew cramped and angered. He gave a huge sigh, retrieved his sword, and gained his feet. There was nothing for it. The pull of it was too strong. He'd have to go find her. Maybe even mate with her.

And try not to hate her, too.

# CHAPTER THREE

There was stupid.

And there was major stupid.

Stupid had been when she'd swum across Rockport Reservoir during a camping trip at dusk. Without any notice to the others. She hadn't worn a lifejacket. Or even shoes. She still remembered how it had felt to reach the middle of the reservoir and float on her back, watching the stars come out, while exhaustion weighed down every limb. She'd known stupidity then. She'd had quite a bit of time to question her intellect while the water slowly lapped inexorably toward the dam, taking her with it. She didn't think she had the energy to continue. And she hadn't. Except one of the smartass guys had swum up beside her and challenged her to race him...

She rarely even thought of that episode anymore, unless it was to match it against something even more stupid.

Like now.

Why, oh why, had she agreed to this?

Jill Johnson was normally level-headed. Loaded with common sense. She wasn't at all like the rest of the group. She rarely fit in anywhere. She'd been the gawky one. The one without friends. Heck. She hadn't even had breasts until she reached her senior year in High School, making every shower in gym class a lesson in humility. She didn't possess much cleavage now, although the push-up bras helped. But she wasn't interested in visiting a plastic surgeon to assist nature, like six of the other women in this group had. She couldn't afford it. She also couldn't afford laser surgery for her eyesight. She'd rather pay for things like rent. Utilities. Transportation. Food.

Face it, Jill.

She just didn't fit in. Ever.

The others in her art group were rich girls on a "Spring Break" vacation to Paris. Jill was an art student on a sanctioned field trip that set her back into poverty because it was a once-in-a-lifetime opportunity she refused to miss. She got eight days to study sculpture at the Louvre! In Paris! It was an amazing experience. She'd been happy to go back on noodles and peanut butter for this trip.

That was before this midnight side-trip, however. She tripped on something, and caught the fall with a hand slapped against the tunnel wall. Nobody noticed. She didn't really expect them to. They were avoiding her. She didn't blame them. Her attitude had been going downhill for some time now.

She wasn't even trying to fit in.

It was obvious even to a casual observer. She wore pleated slacks that had some give in them, a loose-fit blouse with a sweater atop it, and flat-heeled, sensible shoes. The others were sporting tight shirts, even tighter pants, and ridiculously high heels. They looked curvy and long-legged. And ridiculous. Jill snickered more than once at a stumble. Somebody was going to twist an ankle. Or worse.

Shrieks came occasionally as hair got mussed, too. That was amusing. Her fellow students spent hours on their hair and faces every morning. They looked it. Jill rarely wore makeup and usually had her hair up in a clip. She didn't remotely fit in with any group of gorgeous, giggling girls.

She was probably born into the wrong century, although none of the past eras, with their lack of technology or cultural niceties like indoor plumbing appealed to her, either. And she was really fond of plastic. Without gas permeable contact lenses, she'd have been in an institute for the blind. They were really bad in dirt-filled situations, too, but she hadn't another option. She hadn't brought her glasses for a day trip to the museum. Unfortunately, as it was past midnight, her contacts kept reminding her that they needed lubrication. They needed to come out for the night. And dirt was everywhere in these caverns.

Jill stopped. Flipped a contact out of her left eye, and violated several optometrist health warnings by sticking the lens in her mouth. She spent the next few seconds rubbing at her eye, attempted to dislodge the dirt speck before reinserting the lens. Nobody stopped for her. Nobody even seemed to notice as she lagged behind.

A flash of a headlamp speared her, making her momentarily blind. *Jerk.* She said it silently. Somebody else verbalized their opinion. She recognized the voice.

Oh.

Yeah.

That's right. There was a reason why she was down here in miles of tunnels beneath the streets of Paris with a group of guys who called themselves cataphiles. The reason was named Sebastian Rashe.

They'd met in the Louvre, studying Flemish paintings. A small group of physically fit and attractive men had appeared. They'd stopped to flirt, and then actually talked the art group into this excursion. Every single guy was cute... some more than others. Especially the one named Sebastian Rashe. He was really something. Tall. Lean. Light brown hair that he wore short-cropped. Spiked. He had a hint of a mustache on his upper lip.

Oh my.

Even now, hours later, Jill could still remember how her heart had ticked up when he'd looked down and spoken to just her. *Wow.* The guy had magnetism. Or something. He'd made her head spin. He'd made it sound like he'd be with her. Every step. He'd make sure nothing happened to her. She'd be back in the little hotel before sunup. Nobody would know. Didn't she see how much fun it would be?

Jill actually felt the same jolt. Hours later.

Wow again.

Sebastian Rashe could be charming... and then some. Enough that she'd actually agreed to this. She had to. They weren't taking anyone unless they took everyone. That way, nobody could rat anyone out. That had been a heady sensation.

She'd actually felt needed. Desired.

Sebastian had told her they wouldn't go far. Just a little way into the tunnels. She could view the graffiti – and Jill had to admit – some of the artwork down here was worth the trip.

Sebastian Rashe had used his charm on her. He had a deep, baritone-range voice. He'd even promised to hold her hand if she got scared. He'd take care of her. Besides, there were ten of them and only five cataphiles. What could go wrong?

Sucker.

She'd been watching as the girls paired off with guys, holding hands. Caressing shoulders. Giggling. Disappearing for a span. Five men to ten women were great odds, but they could just factor her out of the equation. What could go wrong? Unprotected sex for starters. And then add a moron who couldn't read the thirty-seven pages of hand-drawn maps they carried. Oh. And he should have taken a head count before entering this particular tunnel. Jill suspected they'd lost three more girls. And two guys.

This was so stupid!

Ouch!

Jill sucked in on the instant stab of pain. Unless a person wore the old-style gas-perm lenses, they didn't know how much it hurt to have a dirt particle in the eye along with a contact. Sometimes it started a stream of tears from the affected eye. That helped a little as it soothed and washed her eye out, but it was like a magnet for more dirt. Jill put her back against a wall and flipped the other contact out this time. She was on her way to putting it on her tongue, when all hell broke loose.

"*Gendarmes!*"

All the lights went out. A body raced by, kicking up more dust, and worse. It jostled her arm, sending her contact airborne, and just like that, she lost her ability to see well.

Oh. *Shit*.

"Run!"

More bodies rushed past her, showing the cataphiles could move pretty well, even in the dark. It also showed their lack of chivalry. Jill slid to her haunches along the wall, cupping her hand over her left eye. She was protecting this one. She'd gone with one contact before. It wasn't a life altering situation. She could make it. Depth perception was the real issue, but she wasn't handicapped.

But if she lost this lens...

Shouts came from somewhere to her left. They sounded like they were a long way away. Already. Jill turned that direction, moved her hand, and squinted. Nothing but dark and more dark. *Great.* Somebody had mentioned that tunnel-exploring was illegal. The fine was sixty some-odd *Euros.* That's why someone was supposed to be on the look-out for police. Jill had been a proponent of that idea. Others might be able to afford the penalty. She wasn't one of them. Right now, however, she was all for finding a cop and getting the hell out of here.

"Hello!"

She called it loudly, but it sounded like she'd lost a couple of decades from her twenty-six years. Jill cleared her throat and tried again. And this time she yelled. Nothing but an echo answered her, and it came back twice. She stood, and tried again. This time the echo was louder. And just as fruitless.

This wasn't possible. She couldn't be lost somewhere in the underbelly of Paris with a limited ability to see, no water, and no companionship. And she might as well factor in her limited ability with the language. All told, there wasn't a range in her stupid level for this shit. Jill's good eye was still sending a solid stream of tears down her cheek. She kept it closed.

The contact wouldn't scratch much that way, and she wouldn't lose it. She didn't dare fuss with anything until she had some light... and why? Because legally blind really was a handicap. She squinted and looked about with the contact-less one. It didn't do much. They'd taken the light. Everything was pretty much the same shade of black. The fact that it was a blur was completely inconsequential.

Decision time, Jill.

She could stay here. Wait for a rescue. The others might come back. Another *gendarme* might come by. There might even be another cataphile group out and about that she could join. Or... she could work her way out by herself.

*Hmm.* Stay here. Or leave. Both sounded bad. And then the strangest moaning sound came, seeming to seep through the area from the ground up.

Oh, double shit.

Jill's heart kicked into overdrive. This place was the largest necropolis in the world. A literal bone yard. The tour guide brochure in the hotel room had all kinds of info on it. They had over six million skeletons down here somewhere. And that meant a lot of ghosts.

Oh, stop it, Jill.

Her entire body broke out in a cold sweat accompanied by a full-body tremor. She'd heard it described. She'd never felt it. She was a grounded, skeptical, sensible woman. There were no such things as ghosts. Why was it easier to think it than to believe it? *I'll tell you why, Jill.* Because being all alone in the dead of night lost in the Paris catacombs could trump anything commonsensical. And eat it for lunch.

These tunnels weren't just black. They were frickin' scary.

She wasn't staying another second longer than she had to in them. But... which way? She couldn't just run pell-mell through here. The ceilings had been low in some places, palatial in others. And she didn't know how many turns and twists they'd taken. They even had to crawl through one section one-at-a-time. But... there had been an exit that way. And no arrangements of skeletons.

Which was the major issue at the moment. She didn't think she could die of a panic attack at her age, but she didn't want it tested. Running into the empire of the dead was completely off limits.

She started back the direction she thought they'd entered, skimming the fingers of one hand along the wall while the other hand was atop her head, checking for height. And the eye with the contact would not quit watering up as it felt like each dust speck got sucked in for torment purposes.

Well. Looked like she had another measurement for stupid.

Something loomed before her, spurring more dust. She sensed size. Solidity. Threat. And it was *breathing*.

The next second she was screaming. And that just made it easier to find her mouth and cover it.

# CHAPTER FOUR

*"Cesser!"*

The word was hissed at her ear. It was in French, but it probably meant stop. Or cease. Or something close. It was in a fairly harsh tone, too. Lifting more than goose bumps, it sent solid shivers racing over her skin. Even her nipples joined the fray. She'd never felt such a thing. Every cell on her body seemed to react, sending little spikes of heat through her veins. For several moments, she was in a state of something impossible to define. Was she vibrating? No. More like transfixed in place. Powerless. Stunned.

*"Comprehende vous?"*

She figured that out without much help. Did she comprehend?

He had to ask?

She wasn't stupid but she was in the worst possible position. Vulnerable and available. Easily assaulted. The perfect victim for a crime of opportunity. Of course she understood. She sure hoped he didn't expect capitulation, however, because he'd picked the wrong woman. And just like that, her immobility ceased. Jill kicked, twisted, and even butted her head against him. It all ended with her getting lifted and clamped against what felt like a really broad, muscled, bare chest. Or a wall. And he was only using one arm? That made it worse somehow.

He started hissing more words in her ear, using a very sexy accent. On the third burst of words he finally hit English. And he spoke above the gruff whisper.

"*Comprehende? Arrettez de vous batter!* Cease that! Understand? Stop fighting me!"

She only knew one male in Paris with such a baritone voice. She stopped struggling. The hand atop her mouth relaxed just slightly. "Sebastian?" she whispered.

"Yes. That is my name. Yes.*"*

She hadn't known relief was a tangible force, physically draining and charged with emotion. She'd say the fight went out of her, but that was too cliché. Jill turned into a mass of absolute mush that barely kept from bursting into sobs. She put both hands atop where his forearm was wrapped about her ribcage and tried to mute the sensation. It didn't succeed. She was doing what she hated most here – turning into a vapid, helpless female. Furthermore, she was making him hold up dead weight of about one hundred and forty pounds. And that's what she weighed on a good day. He wasn't having any trouble, either. He wasn't even trembling at the effort.

"Wow, Sebastian! Thank goodness! For a moment there, I was really scared! And just when I give up hope, you're there. Just like you promised. I take back everything I thought. I do."

"You are... English?" he asked.

That was a stupid question. All of them were from the States. Hadn't somebody already asked that? Or maybe he thought he held Daisha. That was a deflating thought. Daisha was exotic-enough to pass for something not created in the US of A.

"I'm still American. Can we get out of here now?"

"Now?"

"You can get us out of here, can't you?"

"Most assuredly."

"And then you can get me to the hotel?"

He straightened, or something that moved her upward a fraction, while his arm smashed her breasts farther upward.

"You wish a hotel?"

"Actually, I wish I hadn't left it this morning. Don't tell me you're shocked that I don't care about the twits I was with? Trust me. I'll worry about them come sunup. And only if they don't show up. Right now, all I want is to get the hell out of here."

"One moment."

He was moving all kinds of man chest against her back without giving her an inch of room to move. She had no idea Sebastian was this strong. She heard a click at her ear, and some rapid-fire French. She heard something about a chamber. Something that included *Suite de Enfer*. And that seemed to get him an unsatisfactory answer, so he said something that included the word *Minuit*. And then *Oubliette*. And she really wished she'd taken French for at least one semester somewhere in her school career. It would be helpful when eavesdropping. Then again, in the pitch-black, just hearing French was a really sexy-sounding experience, especially with Sebastian's exotic, erotic voice.

Wow. That was a really dumb observation.

He finished his call. Another mass of movement behind her must be accompanying him putting the cell phone away. It was too dark to tell, and she was having difficulty concentrating, but she was probably close.

"You prepared?"

Not for that question. Or that voice.

Jill jerked. The arm flexed slightly with the movement, holding her easily. She was grateful for the dark then, as her cheeks heated with what was probably a very visual blush. She'd never reacted to a male like this. Never. Ever. She even felt an insane urge to giggle. Like any other female. She hadn't known she had that capability.

"We will be moving rapidly. I do not wish to frighten you."

"Uh..." *Oh crap.* She giggled at the end of that bit of hesitation.

"Is that... *oui*?

Okay. He wasn't laughing, but his voice was full of amusement. Why was this happening to her? And why now? This was a terrible time to find out that severe sexual attraction equaled brain cell malfunction. She nodded.

Her reply was the spark to his fuse. And he wasn't running. Air rushed past, lifting her bangs. This was incredible. Jill turned her face, keeping her weeping eye to him, while the other squinted against the onslaught of wind. Twice she squinted her other eye open, catching a blur of gray... and the second time, she saw what looked exactly like a row of skulls. At her eye level.

Her gasp wasn't audible, but he must have felt it, for his other arm reached around her and swiveled her, placing her front directly against his, his arms wrapped about her back... and holy hell. Her palms got pressed against massive rock-hewn pecs, while her breasts were smashed against what felt like hard iron bars. If those were abs, Sebastian had a body to die for. Nothing in her experience was close. Not even the sculptures done by the masters of the Renaissance.

He had a heavy heartbeat. It thumped through her right palm with a rhythm that seemed to match the pulse in her own ears. Exactly. That was odd, but not as much as how nothing about him felt remotely stressed. Was it truly possible he could carry this much weight at a breakneck pace through a black tunnel, and not even get winded? She'd never run across such a male specimen. Ever.

You know, Jill...

When they got to her hotel, she might have to invite him in. Do some exploring... strictly for artistic purposes. No artist could imagine a finer model. She should find out if this Sebastian had the best body ever imagined. The most sculpted arms. An incredibly defined chest and belly. Massive shoulders. *Hmm.* Maybe he should have kept his shirt on. This was turning into a highly charged, visceral experience. Why... she was even starting to imagine a nude rendering.

Wow again.

Jill licked her lips. What was wrong with her? She wasn't interested in a romantic interlude. She wasn't even interested in a relationship. And the last thing she wanted was to have anything to do with a model. Ugh. She'd already sculpted several beautiful male nudes, with egos as large as their appendages. She'd been at the back of the class, trying not to blush. The art department had a knack for finding models with very nice bodies and equally nice appendages. And they were very fond of shedding their clothes to demonstrate that fact. Evidently, not one under-endowed guy signed up to be an art model.

Jill had snickered over that fact more than once.

Besides, she wasn't the kind to fall for good looks and a spectacular body, even if it was well-equipped. Yeah. She'd better just stop there. Even if Sebastian was a perfect male, she wasn't interested. She'd never move to Paris. The place had way too much traffic, everything was strange, and she didn't fit in.

No. She wasn't interested in Sebastian. So why was her body giving her so much trouble? She could swear each breath came quicker, every inch of where they touched got hotter, and her heart rate even elevated.

And worse.

So did his.

What a horrible time to have an erotic-themed train of thought. Locked in a stranger's arms, in the midst of the Paris catacombs, racing through a corridor of death. And worse. Cords rippled through his pecs, moving the flesh against her palms as he tightened them. As if he knew her line of thinking and wasn't at all happy about it.

Maybe she should just get to her room, and hope the shower was stronger as well as colder than the usual lukewarm mist.

And then they were out. Without warning, warm, fresh air filled her lungs, while light assailed her with the force of a really sharp cleaver. Jill blinked once before slamming both eyes shut. Her eye watered even more as an offending bit of dirt felt like it sliced. She was flirting with a scratched cornea now. Every blink upped the chances. The only thing she could do was keep her eyes closed until she could get the damned lens out.

Well. That certainly dampened the pursuit of her erotic themed interlude. She'd be lucky if he didn't run from her.

She was probably purplish-toned on one side of her face, and would be stuck with glasses that made her look like a myopic librarian. Not only were they so thick they distorted everything, but they didn't do a damned thing for her looks. Anything romantic with Sebastian went right into the fantasy realm of her memory. She might as well focus on her eye issue. She'd be lucky if nothing got infected. She didn't even know where the pharmacy was or how to ask for one.

She sniffed. His arms tightened slightly. And the area about her heart warmed. It was immediate and physical, and without one bit of warning. She scrunched her eyes tighter closed to prevent any movement. And of course, he had to notice.

"Why do you cry?"

"I'm not... crying."

"Those are tears wetting my chest."

Oh. He had to bring that up. "My eye is watering, okay?"

"Exactly as I said."

"No. It's not what you said. I am not crying. It's only watering on one side."

"Why?"

"It's a side-effect of wearing contacts in a dirt-filled tunnel. And if I lose this one, I'm going to be blind as a bat and twice as helpless. Trust me."

"What is a contact?"

"Are you serious?"

"Yes."

Great. Now she knew the truth. Sebastian was one hell of a man. Gorgeous. Ripped. Sigh-worthy. And just like most handsome guys, he was waffling toward the bottom of the IQ scale. *Figures.*

Jill sighed. "A contact lens is a bit of plastic formed to the shape of your eye. It corrects vision rather than wearing glasses."

"Plastic?"

"Don't tell me you've never heard of that, either. And expect me to believe it anyway."

He made a rumbling sound that resembled a growl. Jill's body responded without one bit of instruction or permission. Her hands even crept up his chest to wind about his neck, gluing her more securely to him. She'd never felt so turned on and attracted. To anyone. Ever. His arms tightened even more in response.

Oh. This was bad.

"Why... don't you just get going?" she whispered, sounding a lot more like a siren in a 1940's black and white movie, than a lecturing professor. She made a mental note to work on her delivery... *after* she handled this incredible reaction to him. Such a thing was foreign. Hypnotic. Thrilling. And almost frightening. As if someone else was in charge of her body, sending all kinds of sensual signals that he seemed to recognize and enjoy.

His legs flexed. He leapt. She had the sensation of movement, the rush of air across at her ears, ruffling more hair loose from her clip. It was a good thing her eyes were shut. If he was running, he was incredibly fast. And she didn't want to know.

Some things were better left unasked. And unanswered. And before she could even acclimatize herself to the chill, they were inside a structure of some kind. The street noise muted and dropped away. The temperature warmed. She caught the vague impression of people and conversation, and then a full sensation of dropping. It was beyond any nightmarish scene. This felt like he'd taken a dive feet-first off a bridge. Jill kept her eyes scrunched shut and waited for the thud of a landing.

It didn't come. The next moment his legs flexed again, accompanied by the slightest jolt as they must be landing. If she had to peg what had just happened, they'd taken a flight... without any means of propulsion. She spent half a second mulling it over before deciding she didn't want to know how or what, either. It could go in the unanswered portion of this experience.

That's when she started to wonder if she'd hit her head or something. Maybe she'd been overcome by hallucinogenic fumes of some kind. Having a dream sequence of some kind. Or maybe she was still in the catacombs... prostrate. Dead to the world. Unconscious. Yet still extremely aroused.

"We have arrived."

The words rumbled through the chest she was clinging to, cancelling out the hallucinogenic theory. He didn't sound remotely interested in her, or her rampant, uncontrollable response. Thankfully, he didn't even sound aware of it, either.

Jill cracked open her unscratched eye. Not good. The place was a blur of space. An ocean of red floor warmed the area. It could be wood. Really expensive wood. She opened her scratched eye, and got an immediate shot of pain lancing through her skull. It wasn't enough to dismiss the obvious.

This was not her hotel.

It wasn't even close.

# CHAPTER FIVE

This woman, his mate was fairly entertaining. That could be a good sign. Everything she said and did was interesting. It took a bit of time to decipher and evaluate her meaning. His current circumstances, for instance. She'd entrenched herself in the bathroom of this suite and locked the door. And that came after she'd cried out, slapped a hand to the weeping eye, and demanded he show her the direction.

He had.

His mate also talked to herself. That was another bit of entertainment. Sebastian concentrated and could hear her easily as she turned on the faucet and fussed with her contact thing, deciding to use it in the wrong eye.

There was a right and wrong eye? Who would design such a thing?

She was very annoyed at him, too, for some reason. That was mystifying. He'd thought she'd recognized him instantly. She'd known his name, hadn't she? And wasn't it her request for a hotel? Didn't that mean she wanted privacy with him? This was very mystifying, especially after the way she'd cleaved to him. Her entire body had been affixed to his during the journey here. Yet now she called him a dick-head who was too accustomed to using the wrong brain to think with?

*There was a wrong brain, too?*

He didn't know the meaning of that, but it didn't sound flattering. He'd figure it out later. She definitely piqued his intellect. Keeping up with her would present quite a challenge.

She was also a rarity. Even to his jaundiced viewpoint, she had a natural beauty. Her skin was translucent and clear. He didn't know her eye color. She'd kept them squeezed shut since he met her. Maybe they matched her hair. He'd had a bit of contact with her hair as it came undone. It was honey-colored. Sweet-smelling. He told himself he didn't care. He was only making an observation. His mate didn't let her hair grow past her hips like Isabelle had. No. This woman kept her hair approximately the length of his. Mid-back, perhaps. She was also quite a bit shorter than Isabelle had been. His wife had been tall and willowy, blessed with an undisguised grace. This woman probably reached to his mid-chest. If she was standing on tip-toe.

Lest he forget, however, she was also very curvaceous. Soft in amazing places. Womanly. Probably moist...

Sebastian looked down as his loins stirred. Grew hard. Imperative. Uncontrollable.

She started talking again. Sebastian looked over at the bathroom door as if caught in some illicit act. He sent the message to his groin to cease. It didn't work. He watched his trousers distort outward with more than perplexity. This wasn't what he remembered. Sebastian Cole wasn't an unbridled youth on the precipice of manhood, undisciplined and randy. He'd been the warlord, Sebastian the Mighty. Leader of a great Bulgar tribe. He was strong in form and stronger in will. He could still prove it. He'd only been bested by one man. And that was in this afterlife: Akron Profit.

The power of this physical response wasn't possible. Or warranted. And it wasn't remotely wanted.

"Well. Might as well get this over with. Sebastian is going to rue the day he thought you were easy. Shoulders back, Girl. Deep breath. And...here goes."

Sebastian pulled his sword from its scabbard and stabbed the tip into the floor before him. He placed both hands atop the hilt, strategically shielding his erection. He was just in time. He heard the lock click. Watched the handle turn. A moment later she yanked it open and stepped out, head back and eyes wide. Sebastian faced her wordlessly. She'd calmed some of the purple that had shaded one side of her face. And she had light ale-colored eyes. Beautiful eyes. They looked golden in the candlelight. They went wide as she looked over and up at him. Then her mouth dropped open to the same dimension. For some reason his back tensed, as if worried over what she might say.

Her mouth shut, she swiveled, and he'd never seen anyone rush back into a room as quickly as she re-entered the bathroom. The door slammed shut. The lock clicked in the tumbler. Sebastian cocked his head and listened.

"Holy shit, Jill! *That* is not Sebastian Rashe! Oh, balls! What have you gotten yourself into this time? No wonder you were envisioning a naked sculpture of him. That guy can't be real. He can't. He's like... the Sebastian you know squared. No. He's more like Sebastian to the third power. Ninth. Oh, Jill! What are you going to do now?"

She'd been envisioning him naked?

Sebastian broke into a grin at the awe-stained praise. And then he sobered. Wait a minute. What was she saying? She'd thought him a different Sebastian? The thought sent a new sensation pumping through his veins. It burned. Angered. And even that failed to dampen the annoyance of his arousal.

Lust had never been a problem.

It was now.

He lowered his chin, set his jaw, and looked about. There was a grouping of large, high-backed chairs situated next to a pseudo-fireplace. It wasn't for burning real wood. Not in here. They were in the *Oubliette* Suite, well beneath the street level. He'd booked it because the Inferno and Midnight ones were already occupied. The walls were solid rock, covered with enormous tapestries in sunset hues. Expensive wooden furnishings decorated some of the space, while an enormous, four-poster bed sat atop a partition in one corner. This room had no resemblance to its namesake, other than the main access point, twenty feet above his head. In the ceiling. This room was named after the portion of a dungeon where they dropped prisoners in and forgot them. It was sound-proof. Extremely secure.

And very private.

This *oubliette* contained every luxury, and if one desired something more, there were all kinds of avenues to gain them. Every telephone connected to the front desk. There were electrical outlets and internet links. There was a power switch that lowered a ladder if he wished to use the ceiling aperture. There was even a real door, reached through an armoire. It led to an elevator shaft and stairs.

All told, it was perfect for what he'd selected it for: mating.

And now everything was changed. He'd gone on the supposition that she knew who he was and why they were here. Now, he had to regroup. Rein back. Strategize.

Sebastian crossed the redwood floor, grabbed up one of the chairs, and took it to the center of the room. He faced it to the bathroom door. And sat in it. He slid down into a slouched position. Stabbed his sword into the floor. Again. And then had to rearrange his crotch area to make necessary room.

This constant arousal was getting annoying.

The door handle turned. His mate stepped out again. Sebastian lifted one knee as he faced her. She'd splashed water on her face and hair, slicking the latter back behind her ears. Perhaps she was trying to look androgynous. It didn't work. She looked even more womanly. Amazingly so. She narrowed her eyes next, shadowing their light brown shade and then she pursed her lips.

A solid tremor scored him, starting at his scalp, running along his spine, shooting through his legs, and then it came back the same route. He was powerless against it. It even made his sword waver, sending flicks of light about the area. He tightened his hand on the hilt, even as he knew it was too late. She put her hands on her hips. That gave definition to what looked like an hourglass figure beneath her ill-fitting clothing. Sebastian barely caught the groan.

"All right. You've had your fun. Who are you, really?" she asked.

He heard it despite the fact that his ears were ringing. He'd never experienced such a thing. This was going beyond annoying. It was irritating. Maddening. He cleared his throat.

"I told you my name. Sebastian."

"Okay. Fine. What comes next? What is your last name?"

"Oh. Cole. I am Sebastian Cole. Your mate."

Her mouth opened. She held that position for a few seconds, and then her lips clamped shut and she ran back into the bathroom. The door slammed shut. The lock clicked closed again. Sebastian regarded it. This time, his newly awakened heart was pumping more than heat through him. It was sending little sparks. He'd never felt that kind of thing, either. It almost overrode hearing her next words.

"Yourmate? What kind of last name is that? I've heard some ridiculous-sounding French names, but... this takes the cake, Jill. Yourmate. That has to be what he meant. He didn't say the other. He couldn't. He didn't."

Sebastian pulled in a heavy breath and expelled it with a loud sigh. Wait a moment...

He could actually sigh?

*Merde!*

An instant surge of something went through him, pushing liquid warmth through his veins. He grinned. He almost gave vent to the laughter, but years of self-control stopped him. This was incredible! Amazing! He'd been without any sensation for so many centuries he'd forgotten how it felt to simply pull in a lungful of air. And just like that, it came back?

He stood. Pulled his sword up, ignoring the notch of wood that came with it. And then he regarded that door. The only thing separating him and perfection. It was shorter than he. It was nothing. A simple piece of wood. With a flimsy lock. He was halfway to the door before she spoke again.

"You know, Jill, before you read him the riot act, and stomp out, you should at least look at his side. And what you're walking out on. I mean, Mister Yourmate out there does send your pulse into overdrive. And did you see that upper body? Holy shit. I mean, really. So he's not the cataphile Sebastian who ran off and left you. What loss is that? How long had you known him, anyway? A few hours?"

Sebastian knocked. Her voice stopped.

"Yes?"

"Open the door, Jill."

He lowered his head and sent as much of his mesmeric powers as he could through it. There was silence for a count of ten. He knew. He'd been counting.

"How do you know my name?"

His power wasn't working? What twist of fate was this?

He stepped closer to the offending piece of wood and lowered his nose to the top crack of light coming from it. "You talk to yourself."

"Oh. I am not that loud."

"I have excellent hearing," he replied.

"Oh, no way. No frickin' way."

He sighed again. Loudly. At length. He could get really fond of being able to do that.

"My last name is not Yourmate, Jill. It's Cole. And I'll repeat myself since you misunderstood. *I am your mate.*"

He used the full range of his voice. Items in the room behind him rattled with the reverberation, as well as sundry toiletry items still unseen in the bathroom beyond this damn door. It took several moments before she spoke again.

"Are you on drugs?"

Well. He'd been right. She was entertaining. "Would you just open the door?" he asked.

"Why?"

"Because I want to talk to you."

"Oh. You hear so well, why is that an issue?"

Sebastian bumped his head into the doorjamb. Twice. Three times. That smarted slightly. He'd forgotten.

"Knocking harder is not going to get you in here," she replied.

"Please open the door, Jill. I only wish to talk. I promise."

"Nothing more?"

"Well... not unless you allow it."

"How am I supposed to believe that?"

Sebastian regarded the top of the door, the little slip of light he could just sense, the feel of her... so close!

"Because I could easily break through this door. And I haven't," he replied.

"Oh."

There was a brief silence. His heart actually stopped before resuming. Sebastian sighed again. This time it was heavy. Almost defeated.

"I just want to talk to you. And I want to see you at the same time. Be near you. It's important. You don't understand."

He hadn't, either. Not until right now. Being near her was very important. Out here was the equivalent of his afterlife: Lonely. The little room beyond this door contained everything that mattered.

"You're not some murderous psycho, are you?"

His eyebrows lifted. "No."

"How am I supposed to trust you on that?"

"If I was, I would have had ample opportunity for murder in the catacombs, wouldn't I? And a much better chance of anonymity. You trusted me then."

"Oh. Right."

"Please," he said next.

"Oh, Jill. This is so stupid."

She spoke to herself. He held his breath. His newly awakened heart beat loud and strong through his ears as he waited. And then... finally! He heard the click as she released the lock.

# CHAPTER SIX

Opening the door wasn't stupid. It was full-fledged insanity.

At least with a barrier between them, she hadn't been assaulted by the immense power of his presence. Or whatever he wielded. Goosebumps lifted all along her arms and belly, while her breath came in little spurts as if somebody had a corset-thing clamped too tightly on her ribcage. And she'd known he was heavy-weight wrestler big, but at this distance he really looked immense! He had one arm propped across the top of the doorjamb. The other hand held a sword that was almost her height, and he was bending his head forward and down in order to peer at her from beneath his forearm.

"Thank you," he said.

Her knees wobbled. Good thing she had a hand on a cool marble countertop. He had a voice to match his killer looks. And a slightly foreign enunciation that made her heart skip a beat. This sort of reaction was entirely alien. Somebody else should be standing here, receiving Sebastian Cole's full attention. Maybe one of the willowy girls from the art group. That might be an acceptable occurrence. Maybe a supermodel. Or maybe even an actress with movie-star looks. Not her. Jill

Jones was full nerd. She wasn't a sex siren. She didn't have a to-die-for figure. She didn't wear make-up or fuss with her hair. Heck. She rarely remembered to pluck her eyebrows. She sure wasn't used to receiving this much male attention. *And never from this much male.* Most of her coherent thought process went right out her ears as he just stood there, gazing down at her, with fathomless dark eyes.

"Um. What... do you want?" Crap. Her voice trembled.

"To talk."

"That's all?"

"I told you. Nothing more... unless you wish it."

Oh shit.

Why did he have to add that? Something was seriously wrong with her. Her throat closed off with what felt like a golf-ball sized obstruction. That made swallowing difficult, and worse. All-of-a-sudden, she needed to swallow. A lot. And something about his expression looked like he was very aware of those facts.

"May I enter?" he asked.

Jill swallowed again. It was more of a gulp. He was giving the decision to her? *Balls. Again.* She didn't know how, but it felt like in the silence they were communicating. Something indefinable seemed to emanate from him, coming in waves that matched her pulse beats.

"Yes," she finally answered.

He stepped in with a grace that defied his size, and stood upright. Somehow he made the aura of space about them, including the twenty foot ceilings, seem normal-sized. She'd already discovered the palatial dimensions of this bathroom. Actually, she needed to correct that. It wasn't a bathroom. It was a suite of rooms masquerading as a bathroom. Multi-level marble countertops rimmed the area. Some too high for anything except storage or display, some low enough to sit on. Polished chrome seemed to gleam from the edge of every surface, while etched glass took the place of walls. There were even separate compartments for the sinks, the loo and bidet, a shower stall that fit at least four, and an enormous sunken tub somewhere in the back corner area.

And Sebastian Cole made it all look small.

Jill looked up at him. She shut her blurred eye so she could see him in almost-clarity. That's what happened when she put the stronger prescription contact in this eye. Things were just a little off-kilter. Slightly blurred from having too much power in the lens. And even that didn't hamper the view.

*Wow.*

This was the best dream she'd ever had. Things like this just did not happen to her. She couldn't even find a descriptor for the mass of man facing her. He was immensely muscled. Perfectly chiseled. He was handsome enough to stop traffic. And he was here with her? In the sculpted flesh?

Unbelievable.

In hindsight, maybe she should have joined the other girls when they'd first arrived in Paris. They'd internet searched all night for 'man-candy' sites that looked more like erotic sites featuring male nudes. She'd found her bunk, stuck plugs in her ears, and ignored them. She'd felt the same measure of disgust when they'd made a beeline to the hermaphrodite statue in order to see a rendering of a reclining nude with breasts and a penis. They hadn't been the only gawkers. Jill had taken a look and moved on. She'd been slightly sickened at the comments and giggles. In hindsight, however, if she *had* joined in on their searches, she might have some comparison for what she was facing right now.

Sebastian stood there watching her, a slight quirk to his lips as if he knew her exact trail of thought. He didn't even appear to be breathing. If he was, it was shallowly. He was just there. Waiting. She swallowed again.

"You're very big," she commented.

"True."

"You're also very cut. Ripped."

"Uh..."

"And you are really handsome."

Two dark-toned spots appeared on his cheekbones. They couldn't be a flush, could they? Men blushed?

"You are very direct," he replied.

That was funny. He said it as if everyone she met hadn't already informed her of that fact, and yet, she was still unaware.

"Well. You are the one who wanted in here to talk. Yes?"

He sucked in on both cheeks, narrowing his face. The look he gave her started her body quaking. Jill had never experienced that, either. Was there really such a thing as instant lust? And if so, was this what it felt like? Or maybe this was the love-at-first-sight stuff that so many poets wrote about. Was such a thing possible?

"Why aren't you wearing a shirt?" she asked.

His eyebrows rose. He looked down as if verifying, and then swung the sword to plant it before him at his waist level, with both hands splayed atop the hilt. And if she wasn't mistaken, he was blushing even more.

"Well?" she asked.

"I... um... was working. I never wear attire when I have an assignment. Clothing might encumber me."

"Really?"

"Yes."

"Why?"

"Things could get messy."

"Okay. That is an interesting answer. Are you a male revue guy?"

"A what?"

"A stripper. You know... an exotic dancer."

His eyes narrowed to slits. That look was ominous. And a tad exciting. Her nipples even hardened to an itching reminder of their presence against her bra.

"Are you trying to insult me?" he asked.

Jill shook her head. Swallowed again. *Damn throat.*

"Uh, not really. I am simply trying to find out who you are and why we're here. That's the normal sequence of events when talking with someone. I think. So. I'm going to guess by your reaction that you are *not* a male stripper. Which means... you could be a high-class gigolo, but I can't imagine how that would be so messy you can't wear clothing on your upper body. Then again, I know next to nothing about high-class society. I think I'll just rule that out. If you were doing that, you probably wouldn't have been running about the catacombs. Yes? Oh. Don't answer. I'll just figure it out myself. Perhaps you're a fighter of some kind. No. That can't be. There's not a mark on you. Then again, you could be a fighter, and a damn good one. Looks like your opponent didn't get in one blow."

"I told you. My name is Sebastian Cole. And I am here because we are mates."

"Oh. Right. You did say that. Let's start with the name, okay? Why don't you look or sound English?'

"What?"

"Cole is a distinctly English surname. Yet, here you are. Not remotely English. Don't bother asking how I know. You speak at least three languages and you don't have a hint of British accent. In fact, you have a really sexy, foreign voice. I don't have enough experience with Europeans, though. I can't place it. One thing I do know, however. It isn't English."

*Damn it.* There went the direct delivery again. The flush moved over his shoulders and into his pecs, staining his tan to a nice rosy hue. Wow. Looked like he went shirtless fairly often... for whatever reason. She wasn't complaining. She actually wanted to applaud. He'd be an absolute joy to sculpt. Plus, her remark had pulled him out of his predatory-looking pose, too. *Double bonus.*

"I chose Cole as a surname... in... the eighteenth century, I believe. I was known as *Der Machtige*, but that raised many brows as the decades passed."

"Right. What does that mean, please? The *Der* part."

"The Mighty."

"You were Sebastian, The Mighty?"

"See. It raises your brows, too. So... I chose Cole. Short. Easy. And I'd just passed a coal mine. When I was asked, I supplied the name Cole. It was necessary. For inheritance purposes."

"Oh. Right. Like that makes sense."

"You've never heard of an inheritance?"

"Of course I have. I received quite a healthy one when my parents disappeared under the collapsed roof in the food court one afternoon. One moment we're eating hamburgers... and the next, a mass of gray-shaded rubble is in their place while somebody won't quit screaming. It took some time before I realized the screamer was me. You speak of an inheritance? Well. Let me tell you. I had a really nice one, until my guardians supposedly used it to have me evaluated and diagnosed, as if I didn't already know I have social and emotional issues. That's what happens when you are home-schooled and then released into the public school system after your parents die. By-the-way, thank you so much for reminding me of all that. Really. Thanks."

He didn't answer. He just looked down at her as if pondering what she said and finding it lacked verisimilitude. *Figures.* She clicked her tongue, shook her head, and looked down at his entwined hands atop the sword.

She felt a tear run down her cheek and swiped at it. "Oh, Jill. Jill. What are you doing? This is ancient history. And bad timing. I mean look at this guy. This is severely bad timing."

"You are talking to yourself again."

Jill looked back up at him. "Oh, yeah? Well. I always do. That's what happens when your mother was a professor of library science, and your father was a mathematical physics genius. I talk to myself because nobody else understands me."

"They don't?"

"Of course not. And it's not an issue. Nobody's ever there, anyway."

He moved a fraction of an inch, his eyes soft. Almost concerned. "I'm here."

Jill choked. It was more a snorting sound. "True. But you are a figment of my imagination, so you don't count."

He pulled in a deep breath and held it. The heavy sigh that followed lifted some of her bangs with the force of it. And what was really strange, she seemed to have made the same sigh. Without conscious thought or need. She'd matched him physically? It wasn't likely. Was it even possible?

"Do I not look real? Surely I sound it?"

"Actually, you sound borderline psychotic. But you do look pretty substantial. You're probably very heavy. No wonder you didn't have any trouble carrying my weight. What do you tip the scales at, anyway? Two-fifty?"

This time he didn't sigh. It sounded more like a grunt from deep in his throat. "This is not working."

"No lie."

"Jill. Please listen to me. I am not imaginary. I am very real. And you keep missing the rest of my words. I am here because I am your mate."

"Oh. I heard that part. I'm just avoiding it. I mean... um. This word you toss around. Mating. That puts a negative, animalistic-sounding connotation to something that should be incredibly beautiful, very personal, and extremely intimate. I mean, if that's your pick-up line, you probably need to work on it."

He stepped closer still, while his hands tightened on the sword hilt. His knuckles whitened, and cords stood out in both arms. Wow. The guy was more than ripped. He was body-builder perfection. He also had an intensity that seemed to heighten the temperature. She was trembling. She should probably feel terrified. She didn't. She felt like every cell was getting an electrical charge.

"Mating isn't something negotiable. It isn't something you can fight. I'm finding it difficult to keep from you, despite any dislike of the situation."

"Am I coming across... that I dislike you?"

"Not after you spoke of sculpting me. Naked."

"Oh! Oh. I cry foul. You're using eavesdropping against me? That is a complete and total cheat."

"Sebastian Cole never cheats."

"Oh yeah? What do you call it, then?"

It was her move stepping closer this time. He was exuding something that felt like flypaper must to a fly. Flame to a moth. Something forceful. Passionate. Magnetic. He was also tensing throughout his frame, causing every nuance of his muscularity to get defined, begging a touch. A caress. She barely caught the move to do exactly that.

"You speak aloud. I listened. That is not cheating."

"Well, it's completely unfair. Nobody should have their fantasies stuck out in the bright light and examined. Even me. With those frickin' doctors. Oh, this is bad, Jill. Really bad."

"Why is it bad? I know you wish to see me naked. It's completely right. And true."

"Excuse me?"

"I was told that mating is an amazing experience. It restarts everything. Breathing. The heart beating. The senses. The passions."

"Oh, you were told that, were you? By whom? An astrologer?"

"You disparage me?"

"That's a big word," she replied. "Do you know what it means?"

"And you malign me?"

"Another... big word. Wow."

Her voice was breathless, and at a much lower tone than she intended. Good heavens. She was actually able to verbalize sexual turn-on?

"I cannot believe this! I did not ask for a mate! I did not want one. I did not need one. I did not pine for one. You don't understand."

"Wow. That's... everything a girl wants to hear. You didn't want it? Then why the hell are you here?"

"Because I *am* your mate."

*Holy shit.* The guy had a voice that could curl steel I-beams. Lights exploded, sending the entire bathroom suite into a sparsely lit shadow-land. Glass walls rumbled and cracked. She knew that's what the noise meant because she watched a fissure in the glass divider beside Sebastian. The crack followed the lily design some artisan had etched into it from upper corner to bottom edge.

"It is so. I *am* your mate. And despite everything... I cannot stop wanting you!"

He moved his sword hand. Jill's eyes dropped to what he was showing her. Her mouth followed suit. She'd never seen an erect phallus, and his was still hidden behind leather trousers. Sebastian wasn't just physically immense. He was extremely well-equipped. She had all those egotistical art models to thank for knowing that much. Her gasp was almost drowned out by the thump of beats filling both ears.

"Oh. Sebastian. Wow."

Jill looked up at him, eyes so wide they hurt, and then back to his abdomen area. She didn't dare look lower. She watched her own hand reach out next, stopping a centimeter from touching. And then she watched it shake.

"You may not wish to touch me, Jill."

"Why... not?"

"The consequences... are vast."

His skin looked like it was rippling over and over with little bumps, almost reaching where her fingertips hovered.

"So?"

"I may not be able... to control this."

Oh... *sweet*. That sounded infinitely intriguing. Totally fascinating. And unbelievably exciting. Her heart sounded like it was at a full gallop in her ears, while she watched her hand tremble a fraction of space from the ropes and valleys of his belly.

"Sebastian?" She whispered it.

"Be certain," he replied.

And she touched him.

# CHAPTER SEVEN

Two of her fingers reached his abdomen, stunning him. Her touch was a physical force to contend with, an electrical surge that was impossible to defy. His eyes watered as a muscle-straining charge slammed through him, arching him backward as he withstood it. Fought it. Shuddered with experiencing it.

Resistance was futile.

And he knew it.

His head went back, his mouth wide, allowing room for his canines to grow until they reached puncturing sharpness. The sword fell, rattling on the tile before it stilled. He slammed a hand to the counter beside him. It cracked. The other hand grabbed for the etched glass bracket on his other side. The wood broke. The glass shattered.

*Merde!*

This wasn't supposed to happen. Not like this. He'd accepted that he'd physically mate with her, but it wasn't to have this much power. And little meaning. Isabelle was his heart. Her face was the one he should be seeing. Her breath the air caressing his skin. She had his love. She did. She always would...

Why did none of that mean a damn thing?

Jill's fingertips had become her entire palm, pressing to his belly. Her other hand joined in. She slid along his flesh, shooting glass-like shards through his skin with each increasing moment. No. No! It wasn't supposed to feel like this! It wasn't to be this rapturous! This amazing. This—

Sebastian yelled in reaction, the sound pulled from the depths of his being. More glass broke, shattering into little pieces that made tinkling noises as they hit the floor. Nothing could have prepared him for this. It was beyond anything he'd experienced, in his mortal life, or in the centuries since.

And he wanted more.

Much more.

He gasped for breath and looked down, taking in every detail of his mate's beauty. She had perfect, translucent skin. A dusting of dark eyelashes. Incredibly deep, amber-shaded eyes. She had them wide. Surprised. Her pupils enlarged as he watched. A strange look overtook her features. As if she were troubled, yet still intrigued. How was this possible? She was truly adorable. His heart hurt him with the force of each thump.

"You... have fangs," she told him.

He smiled. "Yes. I do."

He was beyond thinking. On the edge of control. Someone should have warned him of the power of the mating. The physical need. The amazing desire. *This was his mate! Decreed by the fates!* And joining with her was becoming as necessary as blood. Desire was fueling it. Emotion was the catalyst. Sebastian had his hands about her shoulders before he knew his intent and could rescind the motion. He lifted her. Brought her to his chest and then just held her for long moments, their bodies vibrating to an exchange of energy that sparked into being, and kept growing. Larger. Hotter. More dominant. His entire being experienced a series of lightning-charges far worse than heat. They were infused with passion. And angered, primal need.

"You can't... have fangs. It's... beyond possible."

She panted through the words, but it was her tongue sliding along his jaw. Her lips seeking his. Her mouth reaching and then...

Her lips touched his.

And the world shifted.

Her kiss was a weapon. A curse. A torment. And a supreme joy. A canine sliced through flesh, mingling their life blood. The taste sent Sebastian spiraling. Rising. Creating a vortex of wonder. A moan erupted. It throbbed through the room. It didn't come from a single throat, but both.

Sebastian's head bumped the ceiling. He had to consciously drop back to the floor, when everything about him was soaring. Experiencing bliss without end. Wonder without bounds. He was lapping and sucking and groaning, and laughing. Akron hadn't been succinct enough. Finding one's mate was an experience beyond description. Without equal. Rapture beyond comprehension. Bliss that transcended boundaries. Erased memories. Even shattered ancient vows.

Sebastian tensed for half an instant on the thought, honed by years of fealty and rote. This wasn't possible. He'd loved Isabelle. He did. He had.

He *had*?

"I didn't know... a kiss... felt like this."

The words were spaced with snippets of her sweet breath as she writhed against him. Her contortions sent all sorts of sensory messages through him. They reached his lungs. His heart.

"Nor I," he replied.

*No. Wait.* That couldn't be true. Could it?

He wrenched his lips free. Slid them down her chin. To her throat. Aimed for the throbbing vein just beneath the surface of her skin. And a moment later, he was there, poised atop it, feeling the thrum of her blood as it tapped the vein against his canines. And then he stabbed into it.

Liquid ecstasy shattered through him, stalling his heart, weakening his limbs, staining his soul. He set her on the nearest counter before she slipped from his grasp. She responded by wrapping both legs about him, and then she clenched them, scooting closer. Nearer. And then she was rocking against his erection in a series of lunges that sent his passions to an even hotter pitch. Scorching hot. Incendiary.

Sebastian grabbed for the chrome-edged, marble countertop, warping it as he fought the absolute need to continue. To take her fluid. Drain her. Change her.

No.

He couldn't do it like this. It was too soon. He couldn't take her mortality. Not like this. He had to stop. Pull back. Fight everything his body was demanding. And somehow he found the strength to do it. He yanked from her in a vicious gesture, spraying a mist of dark red droplets onto the scene.

Dark red assailed his senses.

Blood red.

Everything ratcheted higher, shoving him into a realm that contained massive want, desire, and very little control. He tightened every muscle at his command, working to temper it. Harder. More. He shook until the room sounded like it rattled along with him.

"Sebastian?"

He glanced down. Jill's lips were swollen. Covered with dark red. Moist. Kissable. Her eyes were narrowed, giving him just a glimpse of their ale-shaded beauty. She didn't remotely resemble Isabelle. Isabelle had blue eyes.

Or had they been greenish-blue? No. Maybe hazel?

*He couldn't recall?* It was like Isabelle had faded, dropping from the altar of conscious thought into the realm of memory. And he hadn't even noticed?

The growl he gave contained pain, and fury, and something very close to sobs.

"Did I do... something wrong?"

The stain of emotion in her voice was like a blow. It slammed through his chest, aiming right for his heart. And when it got there, it wrapped about that throbbing muscle with tentacles of light-imbued warmth. Cradling it. Caging it.

For all time.

Sebastian pulled in a breath. Held it until his chest burned before exhaling. And then he moved his gaze back to her. His mate. The one being slated for him through all time and space. She was a gift beyond perfection. One he hadn't asked for and didn't think he wanted. One, he probably didn't deserve. Her eyes had a patina of moisture atop them now. And his newly awakened heart fluttered in its cage.

"No. No, sweetheart. No. You are perfection."

Oh. She was more than that! Small, yet soft. Curved. And gifted with the most amazing scent. He didn't have much recollection to draw from, but he caught a slight floral aroma. Clean. Warm. It might resemble a field of sun-touched lavender. He inhaled deeply. And then shook with holding back more reaction.

This was incredible. Amazing. Frightening.

"Forgive me." His voice was a rasp of sound. He was surprised it worked. "It has been... some time. I do not wish to alarm you."

"Oh. You don't. But—"

She had her lower lip between her teeth as she said it. She was very pale. It made the blood staining her lips and the blush tipping the tops of her cheeks especially noticeable.

"Yes?"

"I... it's. You're. Um. We. Well... uh."

Every word darkened the color tinting her cheeks. And she wouldn't look at him. Sebastian reached a trembling finger to her chin and lifted it, making her face him. It was probably a mistake.

"Yes?" he asked again.

"I... know we're supposed to have... some sort of talk... about now."

His entire body pulsed at her gaze. He barely heard her words. He had a difficult time comprehending them. "We are?"

"A-a-about past history. You know... s-s-sexually transmitted diseases. And b-birth control method of choice."

She was stuttering. That made her even more adorable. And she just kept looking up at him. Every prolonged moment giving a plethora of torment. Every breath she sent over him was doing worse.

"I do not understand," he replied.

"I've never... had a man."

Oh sweetness!

There wasn't a description for the feeling that hit him. It burned and iced, soothed and chafed, strengthened and drained. Sebastian pushed upward to give vent to a howl that contained absolute pleasure. It was lengthy. Deep. And primitive. It caused more damage in the room behind him as things fell, clamoring and banging, before stilling. The echo of his cry ended, leaving the sounds of their panting breath. He dropped his head and bent his arms, bringing his chin level with hers. She was watching him with even wider eyes. Beautiful eyes. Fascinating eyes. Looking exactly like molten gold.

"You will never have another, either," he said.

"I... won't?"

"Oh, no. No."

"That's... rather... p-p-possessive."

He lowered his chin and looked at her through his lashes. The lurch of her frame sent it right against his. He reached behind her, grabbed her rear and slid her forward. And if they weren't still clothed, he'd have reached her cavern, rather than the obstruction of leather. Been burrowing into depths. Sliding deep into honeyed moistness. His eyes narrowed as he fought the urge to tear through fabric.

And somehow he got his mouth to work.

"Possessive?" he repeated.

She nodded. Sebastian grinned, uncaring of his fangs.

"Too bad."

He took her lips again, and this time there was something different. Something... new.

His tongue connected with a little spike. Another one. Slicing with razor efficiency along his tongue. His inner lip. Her fingers slid up and over his shoulders, gripped into his hair, and held him while she licked and sucked and moaned and writhed.

Pounding overtook the space. Accompanied by a dark red wash of color. A symphony of tinkling sounds resembling bells. She broke the kiss, trailed her way to his neck, and he let her. Everything on him hummed in anticipation. Keenness.

His hands grazed her ribs, reaching her breasts, filling his palms with fullness. Bulk. And infinite sweetness. She was a perfect size. Perfect heft. Perfect... everything. He rubbed his thumb along the tips, raising hard nubs, even through the layers she wore. Her pulsing movements against him intensified. It matched the movement of her lips as she sucked on his neck.

"Jill. Sweet." His voice was a grunt of sound he didn't recognize.

"Hmm?"

Her purr sidled right into his ears, joining the thumping noise. It matched his heartbeats. Loud. Fast. Angry.

"You need... to divest your clothing," he took several hard, fast breaths before continuing, "...before it gets in my way."

"Hmm."

This time her throaty answer wasn't even a question. Sebastian hooked both hands into her shirt front and ripped it open. Buttons jumped from the fabric, peppering the space with little clinking sounds as they flicked about and landed somewhere. He didn't notice or care. He was looking down at absolute perfection. No. She was better than perfect. The next moment he had her breasts freed of the band-thing she wore, cupped in both of his hands, lifted, and was lavishing adoration to her cleavage. And then, to each nipple in turn. His movement had released her from his neck, and she was arching backwards, crying aloud with what sounded like pleasure, while she latched onto his sides with fingers that felt like talons.

"I should be slow. Gentle! Careful—"

His voice choked off. He wanted more. He wanted to be inside her. And he wanted it now. Right now.

"I can't wait, Jill. I can't!"

"Oh yes, Sebastian, yes!"

Sebastian grabbed at his belt, freed the clasp, pulled his waistband open, and let the trousers fall. The leather snagged momentarily on his cock. He didn't worry about it. She was swaying back and forth, working at her fly, trying to wriggle free. And she was too slow. He draped her atop a shoulder in order to peel her clothing down her legs, stopped momentarily at her ankles before a shoe slipped free.

Her gasps for breath excited him more. Her flesh was warm. Alive. Shivering. Readied. He brought her off his shoulder, slid his hands past her waist... to her hips, creating a support for her legs to grip about him. Her cavern reached him. Touched! The contact created all kinds of sensation before she shimmied away. Sebastian groaned, but she was right back. Easing a little bit more onto him. Then away. Her motions unconsciously teased and tormented, while his belly went tighter. More rigid. His groans harsher-sounding. More visceral. Again. And again. And each time, she pulled him a little more into her, and shook in place before sliding from him. Her movements came faster, matching her ragged breaths. While each time colored the scene with deeper blood-red hues. The air grew heavy and moist with heat. Again. And again. And without warning, Sebastian lost control. He was beyond thought. Beyond containment. Beyond any power of will.

He grabbed her buttocks and slammed into her, ripping through her barrier, only to get clamped by coils of muscle, legions of heat, and such a wealth of pleasure, he nearly erupted like the weakest of untried youths. It took a supreme act of will to prevent it.

"Oh Sebastian. Oh. Oh."

"Forgive... me, love."

His voice warbled. It matched the tremor running through him, making his legs shake. His arms waver. His back tense. While everything at his groin surged and reacted. Tense with containment. Angry at denial. This was unbelievable. Incredible. No wonder mating hadn't been explained to him with any accuracy. There wasn't any way to describe this.

Her legs tightened, bringing her closer. Her arms did the same about his neck. It was her movement that continued their joining, pulling a fraction from him, before easing back down. Again. And again. Each time sliding a little more along his rod. Her movements became a slow, steady rhythm that Sebastian supported. He didn't match her. Not yet. He didn't dare.

"Oh, Sebastian."

Her voice didn't sound pained. It sounded... young. Breathless. And infinitely sweet.

"Love?"

"Sebastian."

Her movements got quicker. Harder. Matching the breaths she was taking. That's when he tightened his hands on her, and started matching her lunges. Slamming into her with a fury that was beyond stopping.

"Sebastian!"

His name was a scream as she arched back from him, her body shimmying in all sorts of ways as she gyrated in place. Sebastian lost any hope of containing anything. Her pleasure thrilled, satisfied, and then it ignited. He had her atop a counter, splayed in perfection, and was pumping before her cry finished echoing.

His movements grew wilder. His strokes harder. Deeper. Wilder. Each one threatening to pull the marble slab from its base. Fiery sensations shot down his spine, engulfed his hips, hammered down his cock, and a moment later erupted. Sebastian slammed a final time into her, the force of it lifting her into his arms, while a cry ripped through his belly, tore at his throat, and throbbed into existence, surrounding them with sound.

He was shuddering and laughing, and, if he had to confess to it, he was sobbing.

And he barely missed being hit by the countertop as it fell.

# CHAPTER EIGHT

Morning brought the sensation of satin sheets. A firm mattress. Hard, immensely warm pillows. She'd never felt better in her life. Ever. It was like an infusion of happiness and good health had been given to her intravenously. Jill stretched with a languid motion reserved for cats, bumped her head against the thick, hard, pillow at her back. And it shifted. Grunted.

Uh oh.

She cracked an eye open. It wasn't morning. Or, if it was, she'd never know. They were in some sort of cavern. There were walls. No windows. Lots of furnishings. A high-back chair sat in the middle of the floor, illuminated by the light coming through the partly-open bathroom door. It was dim, but not enough. In the brief scan she took, she could see easily. But the motion gave her an instant headache. Something was seriously wrong with her vision. One eye was incredibly clear. Like she had a microscope affixed to it. The other view was more familiar. It was the same as when she tried on her glasses while wearing her contacts. It was over-correction to the nth degree.

She'd slept in the contact? And it wasn't the right one? That was stupid. It wasn't shaped for that eye. She might have it stuck to her cornea. She slid toward the edge, and an arm looped about her waist and hauled her right back.

"Where are you going?"

The voice was male. Deep. Shiver-inducing. *Oh yes.* Sebastian. And wild sex. More than once.

Wow.

Jill instantly warmed with the all-over flush. But he wasn't getting away with this. She rolled onto her back. That was disastrous. He hadn't lost an iota of handsomeness, a lock of hair was falling forward, hitting his eyelashes, and he had a slight quirk to his lips as he looked down at her.

"I... need to use the bathroom," she replied.

He grunted. "Wait. I'll carry you."

Jill stiffened. That was stupid. It just seemed to smash lots of her against more of him. And everything on her body went on full alert or something.

"Wow. We need to get something straight, Mister Cole."

His smile widened. He had perfectly white, straight teeth. A gorgeous smile.

"I don't like possessive males. Actually, I don't like possessive people, period. Besides which, I am perfectly capable of getting to a bathroom on my own."

His head lowered, putting his nose very close to hers. The clear eye gave her a view of perfect face. The blurred one made him look like a wash of flesh-toned mountain.

"There is a lot of broken glass on the floor, sweet. And you are still half-human."

She frowned, and closed the over-corrected eye. It didn't do much. "Excuse me?"

"I am a vampire, love."

Jill considered him for long moments while her heart ramped up, and her skin prickled with a series of goose-bumps. "Right. You know... I think I can get around broken glass."

"Well, I won't chance it."

"Mister Cole—"

"Sebastian," he replied, and he now was cheating. He ran his lips along hers.

"Sebastian," she replied, although it was whispered in a low tone she didn't know she owned.

"I notice you didn't react to the other portion of my words."

"What... portion?" It was very difficult to think with him so close!

"The vampire part."

"Oh. Right. Well. I... heard it. I have chosen... to ignore it."

"Truly?"

"Um. I... never address impossibilities. I spent a few too many weeks in the loony-bin. I heard all kinds of things. I learned. If you address absurdities, you simply encourage them and have to deal with even more of them. So. It's a waste of effort."

"Really?"

"Yes. You are not a vampire and I am certainly not halfway to becoming one. That is implausible and impossible. Therefore, I choose to ignore it. I also ignore UFO sightings, alien visitation claims. Bigfoot stories. Werewolves. Time travel. You know. All the impossible things."

He chuckled. But he did lift his head.

"I... have to use the sink now. It's in the bathroom. I don't need your help, really. But I have to put some water on my eye. I think my contact is stuck."

"Ah. The plastic thing you spoke of."

"Yes."

"You need water for it?"

"Yes."

"In that event... oh. Wait. I think... yes. Here it is."

He reached upward, putting his jaw-dropping physique on display as the sheet slid down. She'd been right. He was the epitome of male perfection, and he'd be a joy to sculpt. That wasn't the only thing he'd uncovered. She was on full view to her thighs. And naked.

Holy hell.

This was too much sensory stimulation, way too early in the morning, and way too soon in any relationship. And she was a novice. He was back. He held a bottle of spring water. Sealed. It was covered with water that dripped from the icy bath it had been in. The drops landed on her, making her jerk slightly each time. To disguise all of it, she started speaking.

"You have... bottled water? Just like that? At your fingertips?"

"Apparently, I have access to all sorts of things. Let me see... I've got lotions. Lubricants. Uh... this is odd. A tube of chocolate-flavored body jelly?"

He was reaching again, lunging up, and putting all sorts of stimuli against her. Jill tipped her head to watch. The headboard must be following the theme of the bathroom. It was chrome-edged and made of glass. But it wasn't see-through. Their headboard was one gigantic mirror. It reflected her as a shadowy darkness against the white sheets. There was a basket of items atop the headboard. She watched as he shuffled around in it.

"Here's a packet of roasted almonds. A tin of rose-scented wax. And a selection of these things."

He held a sealed condom package. Jill almost giggled. It was better to stay busy. She sat up, pretending not to notice anyone's lack of clothing, opened her water bottle, doused her eye, steadied the bottle between her thighs, stanched any blush over that sensation, and then flipped the contact out. She was on her way to putting it in her mouth when she realized something completely incredible.

She could see.

Perfectly.

It was better than she'd ever dreamed. No. Wait. It was beyond that. She had ultra-vision. Jill cried out and clapped her hands, and didn't even care at that moment that she lost the lens.

"What is it? What happened?"

Sebastian was on his knees beside her instantly, lifting the bottle from her to glare at it. And then he turned a puzzled expression to her as she started laughing.

"I can see! Oh, Sebastian... I can see!"

He settled onto his buttocks, giving her a perfect view of perfect male, arrayed in absolutely nothing but air. *Oh. My.* This man? In that pose? The entire sculpting class would faint. And her new eyesight didn't miss an inch.

"Oh, Jill. Jill. Get a grip, Girl. Even if this doesn't change, you'll need to get it verified. Checked. Good thing you have a spare pair of contacts at your hotel. And your glasses. Because this... is not... possible."

He ran a finger up the inside of her arm. "You are talking to yourself again."

"Yeah. I know. Supposedly that's a side-effect of Aspergers."

"Asp-what?"

"Aspergers. That's why I was home-schooled. And that's why I am now broke."

"What?"

"I don't have it. Okay? I've been tested and re-tested, and poked and prodded, and just because I exhibit behaviors that some people find odd, does not mean I have been misdiagnosed."

"Mis... diagnosed?"

"I do not have Aspergers." Jill said again. "Look. If you want the clinical description, supposedly it's an autism spectrum disorder characterized by difficulty with social interaction, intense fascination with one thing – in my case, fine art and sculpting. Oh! And sometimes it leads to very high IQ ratings."

"IQ ratings?"

"You haven't heard of that, either? It stands for Intelligence Quotient. And it's all so pointless. The medical community isn't even specific on what Aspergers is... or even if it exists. My parents had me tested. Twice. Both times came back negative. I'm fine. A bit withdrawn and antisocial, but completely normal. My parents agreed. My guardians didn't. They spent almost every dime I own trying to get a proper diagnosis so I could be cured. Or so, they told the court when I sued them."

Her voice cracked. *Stupid girl*. What was the matter with her? She'd had the most amazing experience with the most unbelievable guy, and now she'd gained perfect sight! What a crazy time to bring up nonsense like this.

"That is in your past, Jill."

"Yeah. I know. Thanks for the reminder."

"It's not a reminder. It's fact. You are my mate. We've shared blood. Physical ailments will never happen to you again."

"And there you go again, right into the psychotic arena. Sebastian. Listen. I think you're... a-a-amazing. For my first ex-experience with... um... s-sex..." *Crap.* She was stuttering *and* blushing.

"This better have a good ending," he replied.

"That's just it. The ending stuff. Sometimes relationships work out. E-e-even those based on really great s-s-sex. Like... um... ours."

He growled. That didn't sound like a good sign.

"I'm not complaining... really. I'm more... overawed. Okay? I'm just, uh... working it out aloud here."

"You are my mate, Jill."

The bed shook beneath them. A picture fell off the wall behind him. She watched it from over his shoulder. *Man!* He had a great voice. She swallowed.

"Wow. Sebastian. We really need to do something about that possessive streak of yours if we want a relationship. Okay? You can't just up and claim me. This is not the Middle Ages. Men no longer have the right to own women. Got it?"

He smiled at her, as if she'd said something amusing.

"You mistake me, my love. It's more than that. You see, it isn't possession. It's reality. And it works both ways. You are not just my mate. I am yours, as well."

"Well. That certainly has possibilities."

She was teasing. He wasn't.

"It was a surprise to me, as well."

"You see? Even you realize how bizarre this is."

"You mistake me again. It was a surprise because I was not expecting it. I had a wife. I loved her. I did not think it possible to love another. And to actually have and find my true mate? I thought it a fairytale. I was a naïve fool. I know that now. It has happened to me... despite everything."

"Wait a minute. You're *married*?"

"No. No, sweetheart. I am a widower."

"Was she very beautiful?" And why on earth did she have to ask that?

"There is no comparison to you," he replied.

"You see? Even you realize how incongruous we are."

He gave worse than a growl this time. It was a deep throb of noise that punctuated the stillness.

"You mistake me again! I say there is no comparison, because it is true. My time with Isabelle was sweet. Now? It is but a memory. A mere blink in the span of eternity. She was not my mate. I know that now. You are. And make no mistake, Jill. You are perfection, itself. Finding you is a prize I am unworthy to even grasp, let alone receive. And yet here you are. Do you understand yet?"

"We can't possibly be mates, Sebastian. I mean, honestly. Look at us. Just look."

She gestured to the headboard mirror and watched her movement coming from a weirdly indistinct and shadowy form. Sebastian wasn't anywhere in the mirror.

"Um. Sebastian?"

Her reflection reached for him. She connected with a lightning shock that went right down her arm and into her chest, where it muted and then surrounded her heart with warmth. That sensation wasn't probable. It certainly wasn't physically verifiable. It still happened. And while that was distinct and real – her fingers told her how real – she watched as her reflection touched absolutely nothing.

"Yes?"

He was there. The word not only rumbled in the air, but she felt it reverberate through his chest where she was still touching.

"You're not in the mirror."

Her voice quavered. It was far shy of the reaction just starting somewhere deep within her, coming up from the dark corner where she'd once gone when her parents first died. The place that might actually be insane.

"I know," he replied. "I have no reflection. I haven't for centuries."

"Why not?"

"I told you. I am a vampire."

Jill blinked several times. Narrowed her eyes. Nothing in the mirror changed. She was still there, shadowy but provable. He wasn't. She turned and looked at him. Back to the mirror. Back to him.

"This is not possible."

He choked. He was probably amused. She wasn't. She was busily assimilating facts. Reality. Emotions. None of this fit into any of her mental compartments, even if she tossed out the word impossible.

*He's a vampire?*

From the bathroom area, a strange chirping noise started. It was barely audible. They both turned their heads toward it.

"I appear to have a call," Sebastian said. "You won't move while I fetch my cell?"

"I might faint."

"In that case, I'll just take you with me."

A moment later, she was atop a shoulder, surveying all sorts of damage in what had been a luxurious bathroom. She'd never moved that rapidly in her life. Ever. She watched her reflection in a shard of glass, hanging from a broken frame. She looked like she hovered in mid-air.

Strange.

She didn't feel insane.

Despite the proof before her eyes.

# CHAPTER NINE

Sebastian stooped to retrieve his trousers, found the cell phone pack in the back pocket. Slid one out. The entire time, he was trying to ignore how it felt to have her weight atop his shoulder.

Her naked weight.

Mating was too new. She was too wondrous. Every moment heightened a physical desire and need he was having trouble coming to grips with. His voice had a tremor as he answered his call.

"Yes?"

"Is this Sebastian Cole?"

"Who were you expecting?"

"Oh. I was expecting the Shah of Persia to answer your line. Who else?"

Akron answered before Sebastian formed an answer. He could usually trade quips with Nigel without thinking. He was having trouble with that at the moment. His mate was giving off the most amazing sensation of warmth, and her scent had gotten more enticing. Intense. She definitely smelled like a sun-warmed field of lavender.

"Nigel. Cease wasting time on frivolities. Have you reached Cole yet?"

"Yes, Sir. He's on the line."

"Good. Sebastian?"

"Sir?"

"Listen up. I appear to have made a few miscalculations in your last assignment."

Sebastian frowned. *The private investigator?* "Bracket's dead," he informed them.

"Yes. I know. That's not the part I'm referring to. Let me start by saying I'm rather grateful you used a new pilot this trip... especially one who is too young to worry over the effects of smoking. I'm also grateful that you gave him our number in the event of trouble."

"Ivan... had trouble?"

"Yes. Well. Apparently, your new pilot, Ivan, stepped out for a smoke just after you landed. He is a very good man. You did well in selecting him. He noticed a lot of strange men about. Men who were wearing an odd shade of camouflage and carrying strange-looking weapons. Sound familiar?"

"Hunters?"

"Exactly. They have now surrounded the hangar. They'd have Ivan in interrogation if he hadn't been sharp enough to call us... after you failed to pick up, of course. I don't suppose you checked your messages lately?"

"No."

"Well. I'll just continue, then. That was my first miscalculation on this assignment. Pity. I really like that airfield."

"My failure to pick up the cell?" Sebastian asked.

Akron chuckled. "No. No. I underestimated the amount of intelligence the Hunters actually possess. And sometimes even display. At the strangest moments. That was mistake one. They are now in control of your plane. And they know you are in the vicinity. Care to know what mistake number two was?"

"What?"

"Believing my associates when they say they detest a place. I actually took that to mean that a certain fellow actually did detest Paris. And wouldn't still be encamped there."

Sebastian colored slightly. "I... found my mate."

"No way!" Nigel inserted. "He did *not*—."

"Nigel. Please. Hasn't it ever occurred to you that I might have a slight foreboding that something like this might happen? And that, maybe – just maybe – I make certain associates are in the exact place they need to be? Even if they claim to detest it?"

"You... *know*?"

"Oh. Dear. That sounds like a harbinger to future harassment. Perhaps I shouldn't have given you that information."

"You mean... you know when my mate is going to show up?"

"Perhaps."

"Really? Oh, Sir! That is so... totally cool! Where is she? What is she like? What nationality? Is she cute? Stacked? Can I meet her? See her? Check her out? Come on, Sir! Can't I get just a hint?"

"You know, Nigel. I am perfectly capable of avoiding this conversation until any mate of yours is well into her middle years. It might be considered by some to be a favor, since you did mention something about being cougar bait. Yes?"

"What? Oh, please Sir. No. Not over forty-five. Please? I'm begging here. I can't handle saggy boobs."

Akron laughed heartily. Sebastian's ears rang. He had to move the phone away.

"I do enjoy your company, Nigel. I really do. You are so... refreshing. You haven't much in the way of sensitivity training, and zero sense of political correctness, but you are honest. Direct. And endlessly amusing. Sebastian?"

"Yes?"

"We'll call you back. New phone."

The line went dead. Sebastian pitched that phone into the wreck of room behind him and slid another one out. Opened it. Pressed the "call" button. It went live instantly and Akron was already speaking.

"...and if she's a toddler? What then? You don't want to know. Trust me, Nigel. Ah. Sebastian is back. Do you have your mate with you?"

Sebastian glanced sidelong at Jill's posterior atop his shoulder. His heart stuttered. *Hmm.* She had a very nice—

"I take it that's a yes," Akron said.

Sebastian choked. Colored. "Uh. Yes. Yes. I have her."

"Good. I also take it you're still in the *Oubliette* Suite?"

"How do you know that?"

"You are a victim of your own arrogance, Sebastian. You used your real name to book the reservations, *and* you went through a travel agency. We've known where you were the moment we were informed that Hunters were on your trail. We scrambled all data to reservation desks to every major hotel in the city, and a few seedier places that Nigel picked out. While, that's bound to give some front desk clerks nightmares, it isn't fool-proof. And the Hunters aren't fools. They might not know where you are yet, but I'm not underestimating their intelligence a second time. They sent two of their best after you. Pair Hunters. With a total of eight pair patches between them. I do not wish them to gain a ninth. That suite has access to the tunnels?"

"Yes."

"Good. I have Ivan and another jet fueled and ready at Cobley Airfield. Do you know where that is?"

"I'll find it."

"You do that. And Sebastian? If this was any other associate... I'd be making plans for their wake. Good luck."

The phone went dead. Sebastian chucked it, grabbed up his trousers, boots, sword, her cast-off clothing, and was back in the room before Jill spoke.

"Okay. Okay. You move too fast. Holy cow, Sebastian. Slow down for a second."

"No time. You heard?"

Sebastian bent forward and put her on her feet. And then, despite everything, he stopped for a moment and just absorbed the sight. Oh! Mating had such power. He hadn't known. He hadn't guessed. And, now that he had it, he wasn't letting anyone take it from him. Especially a Hunter. His face set. His muscles went taut. Battle-ready.

"I heard... a lot of stuff. Now I have to absorb and believe it. Let me get this straight. Vampires are not only real, but so are vampire hunters?"

"Yes. Here. Dress. Quickly. Please?"

"And they really do hunt vampires?"

"Yes."

"Why?"

"They don't like us. The feeling is mutual."

"Now, this is really stupid. We aren't just starting wars nowadays, we're still having them in folklore? Why can't everybody just get along, huh?"

Sebastian had his pants on. Belted in place. His feet shoved into boots. His armbands strapped on. She'd donned her hip garment but stopped there to query him with her breast band thing dangling from her fingers. Sebastian had to look away. She was so tempting!

"Please, Jill. We must hurry!"

"Okay. Okay. Say I believe you. You're a vampire. And I'll go out on a limb and sound really crazy by saying I'm halfway to being one. But do I really have to believe in the vampire hunting stuff, too?"

"It's true. All of it. I swear. Please dress, love."

"But... why?"

"So we can escape!"

He glanced at her. She'd put the breast-binding thing on. That piece of equipment wasn't helpful. It actually lifted her breasts somehow, creating cleavage that drew his eye and hardened his loins. Sebastian looked quickly away again.

"I got that part. But I want to know why. Why on earth do they go around hunting vampires still?"

"So they can kill us?"

"Hasn't there been any effort made toward peace? You've had... oh! I don't know. Centuries? Millennia? Whatever the number. You've all had years of battling and not one of you ever thought of trying for a treaty?"

"Please hurry, darling. Here."

He held out her shirt. Waited until the swish of fabric meant she'd donned it. And then he looked. That was almost worse. She was holding both sides and clicking her tongue, probably dismayed at the wreckage of the placket. He watched as she spun the ends into ties, revealing most of her midriff before she fastened a knot directly beneath her breasts. Sebastian's knees wobbled. His eyes went wide.

Oh. My.

*That* view could severely hamper his concentration.

"Well. I look like something from out of a seventies disco show, but I'm ready. What now?"

"Have you ever been in a fight?"

She almost caught him staring. At her perfection. Her womanly curves that seemed just made for his kisses. His eyes darted away before that happened.

"A fight." She didn't say it as a question.

"Yes. A fight."

"I suppose you could say I've fought inner demons. What kind of fighting are you talking?"

"The kill or be killed kind," he answered.

Was that a shadow?

The ceiling entrance had an opaque chunk of glass in it. The hotel might need it for fire codes or something. Maybe they really did use this suite for sex games. Perversions. Voyeur fantasies. He didn't know. He didn't care. Sebastian narrowed his eyes on the vague square of light the opening cast on the floor. Near the chair he'd been sitting in. Nothing was out of place. Nothing moved.

"I'm going to say... no, then. I have never been in a fight. Or I missed that in the school curriculum somehow."

Holding her hand wasn't going to work. He needed mobility, and he needed her close. Sebastian eyed the bed. A moment later he was there, and ripping the top sheet into long strips.

"What are you doing?" she asked.

"Making your binding."

"Excuse me?"

"I have to tie you—"

"What? Look here, Sebastian. This is going beyond possessive. I refuse."

He reached for her, but she stepped back. On the next effort, she did it again. And since she had received his blood, she was keeping pace. But then she ran into a wall, stopping her. Her eyes were wide as she stared up at him. For a moment, he softened as he looked into those amber-depths.

Ah.

She was so beautiful.

So adorable.

So... excruciatingly innocent.

Sebastian shook his head to clear it. Mating was such a physical joy. It overrode almost everything, even fear. "I *have* to tie you, Jill."

"Not without a fight, you're not."

"Please?"

"Why?"

"I have to keep you with me. I have to keep you safe. I have to be mobile. And I will be fighting and killing. I can't just carry you. I will need both my hands free. Don't you see?"

She tipped her head to one side and regarded him for a long moment. And then she blinked. "Why can't I just meet you at this Cobley place?"

"Oh, Jill. You listened but you didn't comprehend."

"Wow. That sounds just like one of my guardians. I've got it. This just some nightmare, isn't it? Something I'm dreaming because of past experiences I squelched. There's probably even a clinical word for delusions of this nature, although what it might be escapes me."

He lowered his chin so he could regard her through his lashes. "Jill. This is real, darling. I swear it. We are facing Hunters. They kill vampires."

"That look is not going to work, Sebastian. You said it yourself. I am not a vampire. I'm half. I should be perfectly safe. Man. Listen to yourself, Jill. You sound like you shouldn't just be tied; you should be in a straitjacket."

"You are my mate, Jill. The Hunters know that."

"How can they know something I'm not even certain of?"

He groaned. "We are wasting time! Trust me! They know. They will use it. And once they have you, your value is limited. You will be bait. They won't care if you live through it."

"Explain the ties then. I'm listening."

"I need you affixed to me. Close. Arms about my neck. Legs about my hips. Rather... like uh... last night."

"When we made love, you mean?"

"Sort of."

"Wow. I'd heard you men have a one track mind. I didn't know it was true."

"Jill. Please. This will work. It *has* to work."

Another shadowy movement happened out of the corner of his eye. It was definitely coming from the ceiling entrance. They might be preparing an onslaught of incendiary canisters. That would mean they'd only need a small opening, such as that window. They might also be clamping hooks about the edges and attaching ropes so they could rappel down. They'd use the entire opening in that event. Either way he was losing time on explanations when he should just grab Jill and run.

Sebastian tipped his chin slightly. He had seconds to convince her. He and Jill would use the hidden door. Bust through the elevator doors. Slam through the back of the elevator into the tunnel system...

"I need you right up against me. Tight. It shouldn't be a hardship, and you can watch my back."

"You're seriously contemplating battling these Hunter dudes with a woman in your arms?"

"Not in my arms. Tied in place. That's the point. You'll be a part of me. You're small. I'm not. I have great range of movement. It will work. Trust me."

With a quirk of her head, she nodded acceptance, but she was still mumbling to herself. "Well, Jill. They didn't call you crazy for nothing."

She stepped toward him. He whipped a strip of satin about her. She leapt up onto him, latched her legs about his hips. He crossed the strip behind him, catching up her lower legs before bringing it back around and knotting it at her back. Another one followed. He didn't have time for a third one.

# CHAPTER TEN

They used both methods of entry.

Sebastian flew to the armoire, hooking the chair with his free arm on the way. The ceiling door burst open, and several canisters got dropped. And started hissing. He opened the armoire door.

"Sebastian!"

He spun. Four of them were already dangling from the opening in differing levels. Another man was just starting to descend. Sebastian cocked his arm and flung the chair. It was stoutly constructed. He'd noticed that last night when he'd sat in it. His blow hit the closest Hunter on the left, slamming him into the fellow behind him. The blow meshed them into a mass of camo fabric, flesh, and blood. The chair careened off that blow and struck the highest man, knocking him from the rope and into the far wall, while a stroke of luck sent a chair leg right through the torso of the man on the right.

A grenade burst, misting the room. Another followed. A third. All of them dousing the area with Holy Water. Sebastian twirled and bent forward, taking the brunt of the attack along his back as he entered the armoire. Shut the door. Studiously latched it shut behind him. He needed the barrier. They might as well be tossing acid. Fire was eating at his back in so many places at once, the pain was indistinguishable as it meshed into one big haze. He'd forgotten what it felt like.

A flash of light illuminated a bit of black space. It came from the room they'd left. It outlined the door and revealed a peephole that looked back into the room. It was followed by a smattering of wooden shards into the armoire door at his back. It was also accompanied by a loud shriek in the room behind him.

"What the hell?" Jill said.

Sebastian turned his head to look. They weren't just using Holy Water. These Hunters had loaded grenades with shrapnel that appeared to contain shafts of wood. Maybe they hoped to get lucky. They hadn't considered what might happen if they were in the vicinity however. That was almost amusing. It also helped mute the pain encompassing his back and shoulders.

A little.

He reached a door. It was crafted of wood, and covered with carvings that highlighted and displayed woodworking talent. Sebastian slammed through it. The foyer he was in was well lit. Large. He hadn't known they might use this area for other things. Storage. Voyeurism. Maybe they even had other *Oubliette* Suites.

He didn't know. And he didn't care.

He pried the elevator doors open and held them. Good. The car was missing. The only thing between him and space was the mass of cabling in the shaft.

"Oh no. No. You aren't seriously—."

Jill's words ended with a cry as Sebastian leapt into the opening, twisting as he flew. He took the blow with his shoulders, slamming through a fake wall, before stumbling. He grunted. Regained his feet. Tightened a hand on his sword. Jill had gasped when he landed, silencing her shocked outburst. He didn't know how she'd taken the carnage he'd just created in their suite or even if she'd seen it.

"You okay, love?" he whispered.

She was breathing rapidly, while her heart was a hammering force that fed his. Hard. Heavy. Scared. She finally nodded.

The Holy Water had dried, taking the burn with it. The holes it had made in his skin were starting to seal up. The pain had morphed into a throb of ache and soon it would disappear altogether. They'd reached the limestone tunnel system that ran beneath the city. It was dark. Somber. Cool. If he gave it a few moments, he'd be healed completely. He didn't dare. Not with Jill. The scent of something burning was just reaching him. Something noxious. His lips twisted. Hunters always smelled like that. It was their bane. This one had tried disguising it with heavy floral perfume.

"What... is that... horrible smell?"

She was gagging. He wrapped his free arm about her for a second and squeezed. Put his mouth close to her ear. Whispered.

"Hunter. Close."

"How... close?"

Movement caught his eye. Sebastian turned and slammed into the wall beside him, causing a cloud of dirt and dust. Stirring the center into a whirlpool was a spear. Coming out of seeming nowhere with incredible speed. Perfectly aimed. For where he'd just been standing. Sebastian reached out with his left hand, snagged the shaft, spun it, and sent it rocketing back. Using reflex action and little else. He'd been so right to make sure both hands were free! If he'd been holding Jill...

A loud cry came from the blackness. It was cut off almost before it made sound.

"That close," he told her.

He didn't wait for her to answer. Sebastian was on the move toward the Hunter, sword lifted and ready. The man wasn't getting a second chance.

He didn't need the sword.

The Hunter was on his back, the spear shaft protruding from his head. It had split his night vision goggles in two. The body was still jumping in death throes. Dressed in black and dark gray camo. Night camo. He had a silver-embossed broken-heart emblem just above his left pocket. Three ribbons protruded from it.

Three.

Akron had told him he faced two hunters with eight pair kills between them. This one must have wanted first shot at him. Bad move. But that meant he and Jill faced another Hunter. A better one. The one who'd earned five of the pair ribbons they awarded.

He had to think. He'd once made a study of the underground here.

The city of Paris sprawled for miles. It didn't go up. This was why. The foundation. Beginning with the Roman Empire, and continuing for centuries, limestone had been quarried out of these tunnels and used to build the city. The result was a rat-warren of instability. According to estimates, there were over one-hundred-and-eighty-five miles of tunnels down here. Eight hundred meters were devoted to the Empire of the Dead. The macabre arrangement of skeletons known as the catacombs. The final resting place for over six million bodies.

He knew exactly where that section was.

The rest was unfamiliar. He'd heard of large sections being discovered and explored by illicit and illegal activity. Read something about several sections that were used as canvasses for graffiti artists. Seen a program on a large space that had been a brewery but was now an underground art exhibit, the walls covered in paintings. That same program had been devoted to tunnels that had been occupied by German soldiers in the last World War. Other sections had been used by the French Resistance in the same war. One particular tunnel led to the old railway system, known as the *Petite Ceinture*. From there it wasn't far to an airfield. If he was lucky enough, that would be Cobley. In hindsight, he should have paid more attention to the network of tunnels beneath Paris. He wasn't certain which tunnels were open. Which ones blocked. He might need to resort to crawling. It wouldn't be easy. He needed to gain maximum speed and distance with minimum risk.

Sebastian!"

Jill hissed it at his ear. Sebastian instantly leapt upward, clinging to the roof while a Hunter passed right beneath them. Too close. Way, too close. The satin ties held Jill in place, and she'd tightened her limbs, making it a certainty. He dropped directly into the space behind the man, and with a sideways slash, beheaded him. The headless body sagged to the dirt floor, spurting blood in a rhythm that matched his still-beating heart. Sebastian didn't wait around to watch.

Sebastian leapt the body and started running. Jill was meshed to him so tightly, she didn't even bounce. She wasn't as close to hyperventilating as before, and her heart was racing, but she didn't make a sound. She was like an extension of him, exactly as he'd planned. All told, she was an excellent mate.

But he'd been so caught up thinking, he'd made a mistake. He hadn't been aware of danger. That mustn't happen again. They entered another tunnel, skimmed along the wall in the next one. This particular one was narrow. Tight. It led to a huge open area, with manmade pillars. There were all sorts of drawings and paintings along the walls. *Was this the brewery then?*

There was only one exit, a large opening that became a tunnel that kept getting smaller and tighter, then enlarging again. Smaller and tighter. Enlarging. Sebastian waited at every corner, his head lifted to scent, his ears and eyes honed for any indication of anything out of the ordinary. Something about this was wrong. Something at the back of his mind—

A metal canister hissed at his ear level, coming from a fissure in the rock. Sebastian raced back, gained a corner. Another. A flash of light and impression of moisture evidenced the weapon contained Holy Water. That was less debilitating than their wooden shrapnel bomb, but not by much. But, something was severely wrong. There'd been no tell-tale burning odor to warn him. No sign of anything human. No warmth from a body. No sound of breathing.

Nothing.

Jill was shaking. Sebastian cradled an arm about her as he waited for the area to clear. She nuzzled her nose against his neck. Sebastian's knees wavered. He bent his legs slightly for stability. Mating was such an amazing thing! Such joy. Such wonderment. Such bliss. And these bastards were not taking it from him.

Everything on him hardened.

"Oh, Sebastian. I'm r-r-really scared."

"It's all right, sweet."

"But they're trying to *kill* us!"

"I know. I told you."

"No! They're really trying to kill us!"

He almost chuckled. "They won't succeed, darling. Trust me. I'm a warrior. Fourteenth century. War was my life. I had a certain reputation. I never lose. Ever."

"But they've booby-trapped the place!"

Oh, she was smart. That was it!

They weren't being just hunted.

They were being trapped.

This Hunter was good. He wasn't chasing his prey. He was lying in wait for the kill. The Hunters back in the suite had been the first diversion, sending him to the tunnels. Anyone they'd come across since, might have been used to direct and control Sebastian's path.

He was being flushed out. Ambushed. And there were thousands of ambush points in these limestone tunnels. Sebastian had perfect vision, but a dead-end could be a death trap. The situation just got dire. And that meant, he'd have to get smarter. He didn't need speed. He needed stealth.

"Jill?"

His whisper sounded loud. It wasn't. He was just fine-tuning his hearing. Focusing on his sight. Using his abilities.

"Yeah?"

"We have to go back. This Hunter is—"

Something warned him. Some inner sense. Some instinct. Sebastian spun them one-hundred-and-eighty degrees, scraping his head on rock. The arrow that had been meant for Jill's heart pierced him instead. Mid-back. Puncturing a lung. Maybe worse. He jerked at the contact. Gasped at the pain.

He finished the spin and stabbed blindly, since this hunter wasn't wearing camo. He was in some sort of charcoal-colored material that refracted light. It was a new kind of cloaking device. Perfect for concealment. Useless as protection. Sebastian's blade went right through it. He shoved harder, reaching flesh with the hilt. And then he ripped upward, yanking his bade out, spewing blood all over the scene. If he'd stabbed lower, this Hunter would have been split in half. As it was, he wore a look of shock on his face. Sebastian watched it go blank. And then bloody.

The man fell, blood and gore covering everything, including his silver, heart-shaped pair patch.

But his beloved had craned her head, and seen. She wasn't gagging. She planted forehead against his shoulder, scrunched her eyes, and shuddered violently. And she was sobbing, and crying, and then she was hitting at him with her fists at his shoulders. Just above his wound.

"Get me out of here, Sebastian! Now! Get me out! Now!"

The injury was becoming agonizing. As if the bastard had somehow harnessed the sting of Holy Water and amplified it. Sebastian needed to get the arrow out. Get the wound sealed. Stop the blood loss.

"Now, Sebastian! Get moving! Get us out of here!"

"But, sweet—"

"Please?"

Sebastian tightened his right arm about her. The pain was leaching into his left shoulder. Toward his arm. Sebastian held her close. Tried to absorb some of her shock. Warm her. Her sobs tore at his heart, overriding absolutely everything else. Even pain. He hadn't known mating had that much power.

"All right, my love. Hold tight."

She did. Her thighs tightened about his hips and her arms gripped about him as he raced endless tunnels. Debated multiple intersections. Stumbled more than once, before regaining his feet. He breathed shallowly. It matched her. He was trying to keep any blood seepage to a minimum. She was probably still in shock. And he was growing weaker. More than once, he had to steady himself before moving on. He couldn't be lost. He wasn't accepting that. They were too close to escape. He just had to find the one leading to the *Petite Ceinture*.

Skulls came into sight. Femurs. Walls of them.

He'd reached the Empire of the Dead. He should have known.

Sebastian's groan carried fluid. He coughed on it. Jill lifted her head from his shoulder and looked toward him. He gave her a smile for reassurance. But then he coughed. And blood-coated bubbles came with it.

# CHAPTER ELEVEN

Jill's face came into view, her eyes soft. Warm. Golden-hued.

"Sebastian?"

"It's all right, love."

"Sebastian!"

*Odd.* It was dimmer down here than he remembered. Sebastian stumbled a final time and fell. He landed hard, hitting with elbows and knees, keeping her from smacking into the floor by a fraction of space.

"Sebastian?"

Her amber eyes were so beautiful!

"My... love?"

The word was a hiss as another froth of blood accompanied it. He should get the arrow out. He hadn't much time. He slipped his blade beneath a satin strap and sliced, releasing one side. Her weight dropped her, despite how she clung. And then her hand moved down, reached the arrow shaft. When she brought her arm forward, her hand was coated with blood.

"You're injured!"

He nodded.

"What do we do?"

"Break... the shaft. About... six inches out."

Her eyes went even wider. "Me?" she asked.

Sebastian chuckled. It went awry as more blood-flecked foam spurted from his mouth. The view was getting even darker, too. Blurry. And very familiar. A glance upward confirmed it.

*OSSIMENTS DE LANCIEN CIMETIERE ST NICHOLAS DES CHAMPS...*

How was such a thing possible? He'd reached the place where Isabelle's bones had been brought? That was ironic. He'd have chuckled again, but didn't dare. He needed every drop of blood at his disposal.

"I can't do it, Sebastian. I can't!"

She was twisting the projectile, sending spasms of pain through him. He pointed to his sword.

"Hit it with... the blade."

She did. And it might have worked, but it was the most intense agony of his entire experience. Ever. Sebastian was rigid with absorbing it.

"What do I do now? Sebastian! Don't you dare die! You hear me! Don't you dare!"

That was amusing enough he did chuckle. He'd been right. It spewed more precious blood from his mouth. He watched it for a few seconds as it soaked into the dirt floor, obliterating the mark of someone's shoe. And then he lunged up, rolled, and slammed onto the floor. The hit sent the arrow out the front of him. Giving him something to grasp. If he had the energy. And the will.

"What should I do now, Sebastian? Huh? What? Tell me, what?"

Jill was on her knees beside him. Her tears wet his face. His chest. Sebastian put his right hand about the arrowhead. His left arm was useless. It matched his entire left side. Numb. Deadened. He pulled. His hand slid off. It took an act of will to grasp the arrowhead again. His body wasn't obeying. He was shaky. Weak. And his hand slid off again.

"Here! I'll do it!"

She grabbed the blood-covered, slick projectile, with both hands and pulled. Sebastian's body rocked sideways toward her. The arrow didn't budge. He would've cried out, but didn't have enough energy. And that was bad. Everything was bad. He began to wonder if this might be his penance for betraying his vow. For putting another in Isabelle's place. He was going to shrivel into non-existence. Right here. Right next to the bone pile that held Isabelle. And he was going to leave his mate behind.

Jill yanked on the arrowhead again. His body did the exact roll toward her and then back. The arrow shaft didn't move.

"It's not working! A-a-and I don't know what to do! Tell me what to do!"

"It's all right, sweetheart," he whispered.

"No, it's not all right! You hear me!"

Sebastian turned his head toward her and focused. She was hard to see. He had to narrow his eyes. She was surrounded by a gray blob of some kind.

"I love you... Jill."

"Damn you, Sebastian Cole! You are *not* getting away with that! You hear me?"

Oh. She was adorable. Cute. He watched her. He almost smiled.

"Oh! You can stop that look, too!"

She shuffled about and then she was back in view. On her feet. She had strips of the cast-off satin sheet wound about her hands as she grabbed the arrowhead. And then she put a foot on his belly and yanked upwards.

Sebastian howled with agony. Death had to be better than this.

Jill dropped to his side. She had the wad of satin atop his exit wound, pressing it into the hole. She was sobbing his name over and over, and sometimes she was stammering through it. He could barely hear her. He was watching the arrowhead and about eight inches of shaft that she'd launched. It flew upward, arcing over the carefully assembled display of skulls and bones that made up the walls of the catacombs. It landed somewhere is the mish-mass of discarded bones behind the decorated wall. It felt like more desecration somehow. More violation.

A bit more defilement to those unable to defend against it.

A glint of something metallic caught his eye. It seemed to fly outward from where his arrow had landed, following the same path, only in reverse. It landed beside Jill, and spiraled several times before dropping. Within inches of his rapt gaze.

*No.*

*It wasn't possible.*

Sebastian reached for the bit of wrought gold, formed from thin strips of gold, entwined into a ring. He recognized it easily. He still wore the twin to it. It was his signet ring. The one he'd given Isabelle. His hand shook more than before as he reached for it. Lifted it carefully. Brought it close to his nose to refute the proof before his eyes.

Was Isabelle giving him her blessing? Releasing him to love another? And this was proof?

No.

*It wasn't possible.*

That's when he realized he was using Jill's phrasing. If she had to believe in vampires, then he had to believe in this. The gray shade moved back a bit. And he easily heard Jill lamenting beside him.

"Sebastian! You hear me? Don't you dare leave me, you hear? I love you!"

Jill was rocking forward and back. Forward. Back. The next motion forward, Sebastian snagged her hand. Put the ring in her palm. Closed her fingers around it.

"What is this?"

"Take... it."

Damn this loss of blood! The pain was starting to ebb, leaving nothing but weakness. He was even shakier. He really needed an infusion. He'd even take it from a Hunter if he had one handy.

"You're giving me a r-r-ring?" She looked it over, almost like he had, and then turned her gaze back to him.

"Get... to Cobley. Show it... to Ivan."

"Oh. Not without you. No way."

"I'll... follow... shortly."

"Oh. You are very bad at this mating thing, Sebastian Cole."

"Pardon?"

"You are my mate. I am yours. I hope you meant forever, because I accept. You hear me? I'm accepting your ring and your proposal. And that means I am *not* leaving you here. I'll carry you first. I don't care how much you weigh."

He chuckled. A slight smattering of bloody froth emitted from his lips. Good. The wounds were closing. She came closer. Inches away. Focused on him with her gorgeous amber-shaded eyes.

"I need... blood."

"Fine. I have it. Take it."

She lifted her hair off her shoulder, giving him a perfect view of the line of her neck. His canine teeth responded. Lengthened. Feral. Sharp.

"I can't take... from you, sweet."

"Why not?"

"It... will change you."

"Is that all? Fine. Good. I accept."

"You'll be... a vampire."

"Are you growing hard of hearing, too? I accept. I do."

"Be certain... love."

"Oh. I am. I agree. Didn't you hear me? I love you. Okay? I'm your mate. And you are mine. Forever. Okay? What else do you need to hear? Hmm? Well? What?"

He grinned. And then he stabbed into her neck.

~ ~ ~

Cobley Airfield wasn't empty. Sebastian snagged an arm around Jill and lifted her against him. His plane was in Hangar Three. There was another jet in the first hangar. It was getting loaded with passengers. Sebastian watched from the shadows, his back plastered to the wall, and Jill glued to him. Breathing in tandem. Every beat of her heart a match to his, in depth and rhythm. He touched a kiss to her temple.

"Aren't those... Hunters?" Jill whispered.

"Yes."

"Those bloody bastards. I thought that Akron fellow told you it was safe."

"They're not here for us. Look."

The small group of Hunters was surrounding someone. Someone young. Lean. Tall. Blond.

It was Nigel.

Sebastian slid his cell phone pack out. He only had one phone left. He didn't bother punching numbers. It was pre-coded for VAL headquarters. His worst fears were confirmed when a woman answered.

"You've reached the Vampire Assassin League. Lizbeth speaking. Name your poison, please."

"I need to speak to Akron. Stat."

"Name please?"

*She didn't understand what stat meant? How new could she be?*

"Sebastian Cole," he replied through set teeth.

"One moment, please. Mister Profit? You have an incoming call. A Mister Cole."

A click connected him. Akron was in a good mood. His voice was even more resonant than usual.

"Well... hello, Sebastian! I see you survived the catacombs. And you have your mate with you? Congratulations to you both."

"Apologies, Sir, but we have a problem. I'm going to need help."

"Really?"

"It's about Nigel."

"This should be good. What about him?"

"Hunters have him. A small group. They're in another jet. Like ours, but smaller. I might be able to rescue him before they take off, but I'll need help afterward."

"You haven't done anything... to alter their departure, have you?"

"No, but—"

"Damnation! I hate this game!"

Nigel's voice filtered through the receiver. Clear. Recognizable. Sebastian pulled the cell phone from his ear and stared at it. And then he looked over at the jet that was just leaving the hangar.

"Sebastian? You still there?"

Akron's voice came clearly through the phone. Sebastian put it back to his ear.

"Yes."

"As you probably just overheard, Nigel is here. At VAL Headquarters."

"But a woman answered the line."

"Ah yes. That is my reception trainee. Lizbeth. She is usually playing on Nigel's video game because he constantly challenges her to a battle of the sexes. This time she's answering the phones because he finally won a round."

"But I just saw him."

"You certain?"

Sebastian craned his head to look again. There wasn't anything in the hangar. The other plane was gone.

"I could have sworn it was him, Sir. Nigel. In the hands of the Hunters."

"Nigel. Could you come over here for a moment? Talk to Sebastian. He's thinking he just saw you. In Paris."

"Really? Sweet!"

It was Nigel all right. No mistaking that voice.

"He looked just like you," Sebastian replied. "I swear. If it wasn't you, I just saw your double, kid."

"Did you hear that, Sir? I have a doppelganger. Now, that is just beyond cool."

"Actually, Nigel," Akron inserted from somewhere in the background. "What you have... is a grandson."

# EXIST

## Jackie Ivie

# CHAPTER ONE

Anso was restless. Fidgety. On edge.

That was disconcerting.

And rare.

It wasn't the assignment. Everything was exactly as he liked it.

The situation carried a promise of battle; expectancy was like a drug. It was night. The hour, well past midnight. The temperature was chilly. Pockets of mist hung in the air. The odds were against him, too. His foes were armed. Primed. They hadn't prepared well enough. He could pick off any one of them whenever he liked. His target was a man the world shouldn't miss unduly. Vladimir Krenko was known for lack of scruples and cutthroat dealings. And there were plenty of shadow-filled venues available. One thing about Prague, it had a lot of shadow-filled areas. The space beneath him was mottled with dark spots. Long fingers of dimness. Wells of black space.

Anso smiled to himself. All he needed was to decide the moment to act. He handled assignments as he had when he'd been mortal. With quick movements. Harsh decisions. Brutal judgments. Each day had brought struggle. Another battle. A warring clan to be met and assimilated...or eliminated and then forgotten. Existence had been so simple then.

Conquer.

Or be conquered.

This assassination was nearly perfect.

He slipped the English longbow from his shoulder while focusing through an opening in the equine sculpture mounted on the roof. It would be an easy shot, especially with this weapon. He was above Wenceslas Square, directly across from Hotel *Evropa*. The wide space was delineated by large historic buildings, featuring a lot of equine statues. That was probably due to it having been the *Konsky* – horse market of the middle ages. He didn't ponder the reason for long. He didn't much care.

Most of the statues were sculpted in an action pose. Rearing. Charging. Emerging from waves. The rare statues that carried a rider were devoted to heroes. The horse's pose had significance. Four legs on the ground meant the rider had survived armed conflict sometime during his life. One leg lifted indicated the rider had been wounded in combat. Two legs up denoted a battle death.

Had Anso been immortalized in statuary, he would have had a horse with both front legs lifted.

If he'd finished dying.

And they'd found a body.

Selecting an arrow took mere moments, as did placing it in position. Seconds more passed as he pulled the bowstring, holding it taut. Sniper rifles were better for distance shots, but he preferred a bow. Always had. That was one benefit of vampirism. He had a lot of weaponry to choose from over the ages, and plenty of time to perfect skills.

Besides, it was always entertaining to create an incident with arcane weaponry, despite the warnings. His *bodkin* arrows were hewn with infinite care, before feathers were hand-strung and sewn into place on the shaft. Very distinctive and incriminating, particularly if he factored in how many times these arrows had been gathered as evidence in the past. And how law enforcement agencies were cooperating nowadays.

The retinue of men that had emerged from the hotel opposite him was assembled on the street with militaristic precision. Their positions were clear. Their stance, threatening. Bodyguards. They scanned the square in every direction, but nobody looked up. *Odd.* Not one of them noted the threat, despite being hired and paid by the man in their midst. Vladimir Krenko was the sixteenth richest man in the world. A man with so many enemies, the Vampire Assassin League had received four offers for his death in one twenty-four hour period.

Anso wondered which offer had been accepted.

Or, if they'd taken all of them.

He grunted and pulled the string just a fraction more. A creak from the yew wood accompanied the motion while the sinew bowstring bit into his fingers. The longbow had been designed by ancient Celts, taken over by King Edward the Third. Longshanks. And why? Because of the bow's ability and range. An archer could launch twenty arrows a minute. Achieve a distance exceeding anything from a crossbow or re-curve one. The arrows could penetrate chainmail. It could even pierce armor.

Especially if Anso launched it.

The gathering at the hotel entrance made a visual target with a large bulls-eye at the center. Krenko was big. Barrel-chested. Loud. Wearing a silver-hued suit that exaggerated those qualities. It even reflected light. He shone as if spotlighted. Despite exquisite tailoring, the suit didn't hide the man's girth. Nor, did it conceal the weapons he carried. One gun in a shoulder holster. One at his hip. A small one at his back. Knives at each ankle. Krenko's every movement put a corresponding definition to his array of weaponry.

He had a barely-clad beauty queen on each arm. They looked like they could use a wrap. Neither woman was armed. Nobody could fit a weapon in the small amount of fabric they wore. Not without leaving a bulge. And those two ladies didn't have any excess bulges.

A count tallied ten bodyguards with Krenko tonight. Nine surrounded him. One stood at his back. They all appeared expectant, as if waiting for their ride. It wasn't going to arrive. The limo driver had been the first casualty of this evening. But, maybe the fellow shouldn't have fought back. As Anso watched, the man at Krenko's back gestured and made phones calls. He didn't act satisfied as he finished and barked something. The retinue moved, reassembling like a well-oiled machine. They started walking. Three men fronted the unit, shoulder-to-shoulder. Then came Krenko and his ladies, the phone-man directly behind. The remaining bodyguards took up the rear in double columns of two.

*No.*

*Wait.*

He'd miscalculated. An eleventh bodyguard came into view. This one was dark-clad, barely-noticeable. He kept to the shadows and constantly checked behind the group as he trailed them. His progress was quiet.

Stealthy. Anso focused on him for a moment. Made his decision.

And took the shot.

~ ~ ~

"I can't believe you talked me into a ghost tour. Everyone knows there is no such thing. *Especially* psychologists with a lot of schooling behind them and years of private practice." Leah rubbed her hands along her arms, trying for warmth.

"Are you calling us old?"

Her companion had been her best friend since grammar school. They'd gone to college together. Graduated *Magna Cum Laude*. Opened a joint practice that was prospering quite nicely. He wasn't aging as well as Leah, but nothing on him looked old. Or tired. Or cold. Mainly because he wore a man's woolen suit.

And she didn't.

Leah smirked. "No. I'm calling us thirty-four. And way too mature for this. I'm serious. I truly can't believe you talked me into it."

"Give me some credit, love. It took a half bottle of premium vodka and a lot of persuasion. *And* I had to buy the tickets."

"I'm not in the mood, Steven. Your attempts at 'funny-funny-ha-ha' went out with that trek over ankle-twisting cobblestones. And for what? To see a supposedly haunted alehouse that had a lot of aromatic spirits hanging around the place, but nothing ethereal. Or remotely scary. That proves my last theory. They hire these tour guides for their acting ability. Face it."

"That was almost an hour ago."

"My point exactly. It's close to one o'clock. In the morning. In the Czech Republic. Even if they say it's a really warm spring, it's beyond chilly. It's late. I'm tired. We have a class that starts at eight. That's why we came. We paid some big bucks to attend the psychologist convention in Prague. We're here on business. Remember?"

"You need more vodka."

"Oh. Funny. Funny. Ha. Ha," Leah replied.

"Buck up. The tour is almost over."

"And then what? We have an eighty block hike back to our hotel. Or...did you arrange a ride? Please tell me you did."

"Quit exaggerating. It's more like eight. Look at your map."

"Eight? Might as well be eighty. Do you realize how cold it is? And how miserable these shoes are?"

"Grumble. Grumble. You know...most people wear sensible attire on a walking tour. It's a physical comfort thing. You were warned beforehand to change."

"After the fourth drink! You're a sadist, Steven. I should have warned your wife before it was too late for the poor woman."

"She's immune. Hurry! We're lagging behind!"

"Did I forget to mention this stupid, spandex girdle-thing? And you want me to hurry? I'm being pinched in half and having trouble breathing."

"You're wearing a girdle?"

"Oh. Crap. Forget I said anything, okay?"

"Oh. No way. Not an opening like that. I didn't even think they still made girdles. Seriously?"

"It's a specialty thing. From the Goddess Store on Tenth. They're supposed to carve inches off your frame and smooth out bulges like muffin tops. And I can't believe I'm telling you this. Promise you won't tell anyone."

"You might have to buy my silence."

"How much do you want?"

He grinned. Steve had always had a killer grin. "Why in the hell are you wearing it?"

"Because I'm overweight."

"Bullshit."

"The BMI lists me as obese."

"The BMI lists everyone like that! My younger brother is a firefighter. You've seen him. He's obese on that stupid scale. Does he look obese to you?"

"Your brother is six-foot-two of muscled gorgeousness. It's hard to believe you are related."

"Oh. Ouch."

"Besides, your example is way off base. Your brother has a foot of height on me. And testosterone."

"I'll try another tack. How about this one? You are not overweight. You're curvy. Men like curves. I should know. I am one."

"That's not what my last boyfriend said."

"The guy was an ass. You should look higher for social contacts."

"Ronald owned his own construction company."

"So?"

"My social calendar is not so full that I turn down good-looking men who own their own businesses. And their own homes. And don't live with their parents."

"Sounds like an egomaniac. Way too full of himself. He was probably middle-aged, too."

"Forty-one."

"Like I said—"

"Why should I believe anything you say, anyway? You're a psychologist. It's your job to help people see beyond self-esteem issues."

"Can I ask one question?"

"If you don't try and analyze anything."

"Did you gain weight after Ron asked you out?"

Leah sighed. "You're going to try and analyze it, aren't you? And I just said—"

"I'm going to say that's a 'no'. You haven't gained any weight. That means he knew your dimensions when you began seeing each other. Am I right?"

"Is this going somewhere constructive?"

"I'm just trying to ascertain what made the man tick. If you were a certain size when he started seeing you, isn't that what he wanted? Or...was he trying to improve you? Maybe you were another building project?"

"That's it. You're fired as my analyst. I'd rather talk to a wall. Now, can we move onto something else? Like my sore feet?"

"Get your ex into the office. I'll give him a self-esteem issue so severe he'll have trouble asking a woman out, let alone discussing her weight. And...you're not crying, are you?"

"Shut up. Or I'm going to hike the eighty-eight blocks back to the hotel without you. And really be pissed when I get there."

"Eight."

"So. We have one more place to see? Yes? Some church?"

"Reputedly the most haunted one in Europe."

"Please. Spare me."

"Come on already. You love gothic stuff, and this one is...really sweet. Just look."

Leah looked up a mountain of stone steps facing them. There was a yellow-toned arched entrance at the top. The rest of the tour group was nearly there already. "Would you look at those stairs?" Her shoulders sagged.

"I could carry you. I mean, I may not be my brother, but I might have some firefighter physique in here somewhere. Hey. I just remembered. He broke up with his fiancée last month. Want me to set you up?"

Leah shot him a glance. "Jerk."

"Ah!" His finger went up. "Made you smile."

They started up the steps. By the tenth one, Leah knew she was in trouble. Her designer shoes had four inch heels, a one inch platform, and too small of a toe box. They looked nice. Made her legs looks even nicer. Which was why she'd bought them in the first place. And she was limping.

There was a plateau at each twelfth step, complete with stone-carved benches at the sides. They were difficult to see in the shadows. Eerie as all get-out. And heaven-sent.

"Oh! Look! I have been saved!"

Leah headed toward a bench with alacrity. Sat on stone that sent a shock of cold through her buttocks. She ignored it for the most part, slipped off a shoe, and started rubbing her foot.

"What are you doing?" Steve asked.

"What does it look like?"

"We're only a fifth of the way up!"

"Go without me. Save yourself."

"You should have been a drama major. Not a psychologist."

"I'm serious, Steven. I'm not moving another step. Take a video for me if they'll allow it."

"I can't just leave you here!"

"Why not?"

"You're a woman. This is a big city. Formerly Eastern Bloc. All kinds of things might happen."

"Nobody will even see me. And you'll be back this way in minutes. Besides...isn't that Wenceslas Square just over there?" She pointed at a lighted area behind another row of buildings.

"I'll stay with you."

"And miss the tour?"

Steve looked longingly toward the archway. The rest of the tour group had disappeared inside.

"Oh, go on," Leah prompted. She put her shoe back on and took off the other one. Did the same ministration to her instep. "I'll be fine."

"At least take my coat." He shrugged it off and handed it to her.

"You sure?"

"Take it before I change my mind."

Leah took it. Snuggled into warm fabric that was long enough she tucked some of it beneath her backside. "I didn't know you had a chivalrous side."

"Me, either. You sure you'll be okay? You'll stay right here?"

"Yes, Dad. I promise I'll keep totally to myself. Unless my wishes come true and a tall, dark, and extremely gorgeous man happens by to sweep me off my feet. Then, I've got to tell you. All bets are off."

"There's a can of pepper spray in the left pocket."

Leah patted the bulge. "You have pepper spray? That's a surprise."

"Maybe I should give you my knife."

"Steven Bates. I'm a grown woman. Educated. Feisty. Armed with pepper spray. If I'm not here it's because I got a better offer than an eighty block hike back to our hotel. Now, go. You're missing the tour."

"Just make sure your gorgeous man likes curves first."

He saluted. Turned. And sprinted up the stairs, reaching the top in moments. She hadn't known he was that physically fit. Nor had she realized how much his companionship had altered the elements. The stone steps were truly eerie. Silent. A slight breeze lifted strands of hair and sent dirt and old leaves across the steps.

And then a scream split the night.

# CHAPTER TWO

Anso couldn't believe it. He'd taken Krenko with his lone shot. He hadn't created a conflict. Been involved in battle. Taken on uneven odds. Gloried in a fight. He hadn't received one bit of blood spatter when he was usually covered in gore.

His action was completely unfathomable.

He took a deep breath before jumping from the building. Exhaled heavily as he landed, barely missing a puddle. This hit was completely out of character. He wasn't covert and silent. He liked the pandemonium of combat. The excitement of taking on armed foes. The thrill of victory.

He didn't know what was wrong with him.

There had been a lot of power behind his shot, however. The arrow had nearly split Krenko's skull before slamming the man's body against a brick wall. He was probably still pinned there. The woman between him and the wall had been smashed in place. The other one started screaming. More than one bodyguard had pulled a gun and fired it. Their weapons were equipped with silencers. Laser sights. They fired at nothing. No one had even seen him.

Anso pulled in another breath, expanding his chest with it. Slung the bow back over his shoulder. Resettled the sword he carried in a scabbard at his hip. Pulled on his leather neck-guard. Grimaced as his heart stirred with a grinding motion deep in his chest. The motion sent a throb of ache through him.

And that's when his eyes went wide.

He didn't exhale as much as lose his breath. His knees shook before he dropped to one, stopping a complete fall with an outstretched arm. His sword smacked against cobblestones. His knife followed as it clattered to the street. The bow slid forward, stopped by his elbow. And none of that meant a damn thing.

*Because it was happening!*

To him!

Here. On a dark vacant street. In Prague, Czech Republic.

Anso took another deep breath, smiling widely as his chest expanded with it. His heart sent another heavy beat through his chest, this one less painful. He waited. Counted. It seemed to take forever, but within the count of forty, he experienced another heartbeat. The next one came at twenty. The next was even closer. They were growing stronger, as well. This was as incredible as it was unbelievable. He'd thought the stories mere fairytales. The gift of reanimation a myth. And yet...

It was true!

He was being renewed. Because he had a mate. And she was here. Somewhere!

Anso almost gave vent to the shout of joy. Several things stopped him. There was a lot of activity happening in the square he'd just left. Sounds hadn't ceased with the woman's scream. Shouts and yells permeated the night. A car horn honked somewhere.

Wailing of sirens came next. All of it loud. Garnering attention. Nothing he wanted. Not now. He needed to focus.

And hunt.

Anso pulled in another breath, retrieved his dagger, regained his footing, and jostled weaponry as he resettled it. He frowned as he looked down vacant, shadow-pitted streets. Every direction looked the same. And just as empty. Prague was a large city. Historically important to before the time of the Holy Roman Emperor. It had been a labyrinth of dark streets when he'd first seen it. It was worse now.

He didn't have an inkling of how to find her.

Forgetting everything, he flung his head back and howled his frustration into the night.

~ ~ ~

*Okay.*

Ghost tours with over-acting guides were one thing. The cry that had just split the night was something else. Ghosts didn't exist. And creatures that sounded like werewolves were complete and utter fantasy.

Thinking through the facts didn't help. The sound from that cry reverberated off the stone about her before it dissipated. A shiver raced up her spine, lifting hairs at the nape of her neck. That was unpleasant.

Leah shoved her foot back into the shoe and stood, and when that wasn't sufficient, she climbed atop the bench and craned her neck. Even from that vantage, there wasn't much to see. The lighting was pathetic, but the street appeared empty of occupants. Hazy fingers of fog were creeping along the cobblestones below her, just starting to obscure the view. The night seemed colder, all of a sudden, too. She was eternally grateful to Steve for his coat. It wasn't enough, but her linen skirt-suit was useless for warmth. The silk top beneath it was worse. It wasn't her fault. She'd dressed for an indoor event, not this nonsense. This suit made her feel elegant. Look sophisticated, yet business-like. It exactly matched the personae she wished to project at a business conference. She hadn't known she'd be outside in the dead of night. Blocks away from her hotel bed, as well as all the blankets she could pile atop it.

*Damn Steve.*

*No. Damn vodka.*

She hadn't even worn hosiery. Bare legs were getting the brunt of the chill. Maybe she should sit again, pull her legs up to her chest, and wrap Steve's coat about her. That might work at keeping out the elements. It was better than standing indecisively—

"The gods be praised. I have found you."

The voice was deep. Emotion-charged. And pretty damned close. Leah's head came up. Her eyes strained to see. Her breath caught. There was a man standing before her. His feet and lower legs were in shadow. The rest of him was framed by a thin veiling of mist. His head was just beneath hers, showing his height.

*Holy crap.*

She hadn't been this specific with Steve on her wish requirements, but she hadn't known a man like this was on the menu.

Or even existed.

He was tall. Dark-haired. And beyond gorgeous. Leah had experience with handsome men, but never one this handsome. The guy was actually beautiful. So, beautiful, it was difficult to look at his face without blushing. But nowhere was safe! Every bit of him was spectacularly male. It was impossible not to notice the extent of it. He wasn't wearing much, and he wore it extremely well.

And Prague just became her favorite city.

*Oh. Sweetness.*

She'd never even seen pecs and abs like those on display right in front of her. His arms matched. All kinds of muscle flexed as he lifted an arm to push the top of an archer's bow into position behind his head. He regarded her solemnly when he'd finished. Several seconds ticked by. And then he nodded as if she'd asked something.

Her heart stuttered. Her knees wobbled. The heels clacked against the stone bench with the motion. Leah coughed. Tried to speak.

"Um..." Her voice stopped.

"What is your name?"

He leaned his head back slightly after asking, placed one hand atop what looked like a sword hilt, and flexed all kinds of things throughout his chest and belly. And worse. He had a slight accent coloring his words. She couldn't place it, but it made everything he said have a sinfully smooth timbre. Old-World decadence in sound.

"Uh," Leah answered.

He waited expectantly. Leah's heart ticked up another notch.

"My name is Anso," he offered.

She opened her mouth. Nothing came out. She shut it again.

"It means 'god'."

Leah's eyebrows lifted and she blinked several times in disbelief. Her mind finally decided to assist with this. She could almost feel it clicking into gear. She still couldn't look at his face for any length of time. Her eyes flitted to his nose area before dropping to the leather armor-thing he wore about his neck. But staring there was dangerous, too. That particular piece of apparel made a directional arrow pointing downward to a chiseled six-pack-plus of belly. From there she got a full view of really long legs. Encased in what looked like black leather slacks that didn't have much give to them. And if what she glimpsed was real...

Leah yanked her gaze back up. Suffered an all-over, full-body blush. Focused on his leather neck thing. She felt like a pre-teen at her first co-ed dance. Tongue-tied. Gauche. Beyond awkward. There was one benefit, however. She wasn't cold anymore. Leah cleared her throat and spoke. She didn't resemble a clinical psychologist with a waiting list of patients. She sounded breathless. Young.

Smitten.

*Damn it.*

"Um. What kind of parent...names their child such a name? Aside from a music superstar, I mean?"

"It wasn't my birth name." He tightened his hand on his sword hilt, making the muscles in his arm flex, while something in his attire creaked. "I earned it."

"Oh," she said aloud. *Wow,* her mind added.

"And now, you will tell me yours?"

"My what?"

"Name."

"Oh. Yeah. It's Leah."

"Lee. Ah."

He said it with a distinct gap between the syllables and a lot of bass tones. She'd been named after a great-aunt. Leah remembered her great-aunt having purplish-tinted white hair. A long, thin nose. Spectacles. Lots of cats. Leah hadn't been fond of her given name. The way Anso said it changed everything. Her name suddenly sounded illicit. Exciting. Almost breath-taking. His voice sent a plethora of shivers racing along her spine; this time they were completely pleasant. It also sparked a series of reactions through her belly, despite the girdle's grip on the vicinity. The sensation sent tingles. Closed off her throat. Puckered her nipples against their lace-bedecked bra cups.

He lifted the hand that wasn't holding his sword hilt and stepped closer, sending shadow all the way to mid-chest, but that didn't mute much of anything. His eyes sought hers and despite the misgivings, Leah locked gazes with him. Her ears rang. Her breath hitched. She could easily swoon. She couldn't tell his eye color, but they were dark. Fathomless. Mesmeric. His proximity had a sensation to it, too. As if she stood near a massive power source. It raised goose bumps all along her skin.

"Come. Take my hand."

Leah stepped back a fraction. She didn't know how much space she had, and couldn't seem to move her eyes to check. But falling off the back of the bench was not a viable option. The embarrassment potential was too high.

"How about a...no?" she managed to reply.

"No?"

She was amazed the word had made it out of her mouth, but Anso looked as surprised as it sounded. Maybe he wasn't used to women who told him no.

Or anyone who did.

"Please?" he asked next.

"I'm not sure that's...a good idea."

"You exist. I have found you. It is—. Ah! I cannot describe it. I cannot think clearly! Please? You must come with me."

"I've got a better idea. Why don't we make it a date? Tomorrow evening. No. Wait. It's after midnight. Tonight! You could pick me up at my hotel. We could have a nice supper..."

He shook his head.

"What does that mean?"

"Didn't you hear me? I just found you!"

His tone lifted more than goose bumps. It sent a prickle of tears to her eyes, and that was just nonsensical. She wasn't an emotional type. And they'd just met. This encounter was truly weird, and getting weirder by the moment. The mist had gotten a lot thicker, having risen while they conversed. Tendrils of it wrapped about them, isolating them in a layer of white-cast fog. It should have chilled. It didn't. There was a strange throb in the air, too. Her entire body sensed the beat.

And swayed to it.

Leah shook her head. This was ridiculous. She needed to get control of the situation before worse things happened. And if anything on her body obeyed, she already would have.

"Take my hand, Leah. I beg you."

"Um..."

"You do not understand!"

"That is an understatement."

"I am trying to act...civilized."

Leah nearly laughed at how crazed that sounded. Something stopped her. It had a lot to do with the strange aura that encased them. His seriousness. And the way his upper lip had lifted on the last word.

"You hesitate without reason. I will not harm you. You have my word. Now. Take my hand. Please?"

"I...shouldn't."

*Shouldn't?*

What was wrong with her? She'd just used a passive word, one that could easily be construed as tacit approval. There was no excuse. She was a self-assured woman with a can of pepper-spray at her disposal.

"Why not?" He didn't ask it as much as demand.

"I don't know you. You don't know me."

"I am Anso. You are Leah."

This was beginning to resemble a Tarzan script. He moved even closer. Sparks flashed along her skin with the proximity. Every cell on her body got a strong dose of something vast. Necessary.

Addictive.

"Anso...um. It's...really late."

"I am unwilling to lose even a moment from you."

*Oh. Wow.* How many times had she wished her ex had said something like that? Leah didn't bother thinking it through. The number was astronomical. And – why was she thinking of Ron at a time like this? The man might have his own company and his life in order, but he didn't remotely resemble the masculine god standing in front of her.

Now that she thought of it. Anso was probably a perfect name.

"Um..." The word vibrated through her throat. It wasn't followed up by anything else.

"I will not ask again."

His voice lowered into a deeper range. The last words were growled. Leah had never come up against such a blatant chauvinist. Nor, someone as manly. Anso was an alpha male to an infinite degree. She had patients with these traits, but nothing near as ingrained or apparent. And if anything was normal about this, she wouldn't be swaying on her tiptoes in these heels, experiencing flickers of heat lick their way through her belly, upper thighs, and breasts at his words. Tone. Meaning.

And worse. When she answered, her voice seemed to contain all of the sensations afflicting her in audible form. She'd never sounded quite so...excited. Aroused. Sexual.

"I...think you have the wrong—!"

Her words choked off as he lunged. His arms swooped about her, carrying her with him into the fog.

And Leah hadn't even cried out.

# CHAPTER THREE

His mate radiated life. Warmth. Succor. Her presence was a beacon in a heretofore dark world; a haven of shelter in the midst of winter storms; a wealth of heat in a span of ice. An aura of light seemed to surround her. He'd seen it the moment he'd gone airborne. He'd been worried over finding her? That had been naïve and foolish.

If pleasure filled him at being near and basking in her warmth, there was no descriptor for how it felt to clasp her to him. Experience her every breath as they feathered across his chest. Listen to her beating heart as it pulled his into synchronicity with it. Inhale her perfect blend of vanilla and mint. Feel the slide of hair strands along his shoulders. Chin. Against his cheeks...

Anso tightened his arms about her, twirled until the night spun, and then launched forward again. He had to get her to his castle. Hidden. Secure. Private.

Those words matched his castle. It had been built for defense. He didn't know when it had been started, or against what foes. There had been too many over the centuries. But, at some point, the edifice had been abandoned and left to decay. Ownership had come at a pittance. Rebuilding and adding had emptied his coffers at the time. Because he'd wanted perfection: the best craftsmen, finest materials, unparalleled luxury and beauty.

He'd believed he was erasing his origins, overwriting the barbaric portion of his personality with something better. More refined. Much more civilized. He knew the real reason now.

He'd created the castle for her.

The thought brought a burst of something approaching worry. His belly dropped. He lost a corresponding amount of elevation. He'd been extremely short-sighted, but he hadn't known the stories of mating were true. Or that she would just appear one night. There hadn't been one warning. Not even a hint! If there had, he would have prepared his home. Seen to altering décor that was centuries old. His unused kitchens were archaic; the bedroom suites even older.

And he was taking his mate there?

Anso gripped her tighter. His breath hitched as she gave a soft sigh. Air brushed his throat. The sensation sent all kinds of stimuli he tried to ignore. His canines joined the fray, tingling as they started sharpening. He forced them back. Ordered his mind to concentrate on the castle...and her impression of it. Perhaps he was over-thinking this. His mate could always redecorate and update things.

Women liked that.

*Didn't they?*

Oh. How did he know? He hadn't been with a woman in centuries. And, just like that, he lost his thought process again. His fangs reacted. His body spun. It wasn't possible to stay immune to this. Mating had too much power. The feelings created within him were already vast. And they were ever multiplying. His veins throbbed with renewed energy. Power. Life-force. Pumped through him with every heartbeat. Each breath added to the plethora of commotion within him. Every moment sent another burst of renewed sensation. His thighs felt the fire next. His buttocks.

And then his groin.

Anso sucked in a breath with the shock and marvel. He was stirring! His rod elongating. Growing hard and thick against the obstruction of leather trousers. And he felt every bit of it!

Oh!

He needed to get her to his castle.

Rip off clothing.

Find a bed.

*Forget a bed.* He had tables. Sofas. Carpet-strewn floors...

Anso's concentration vanished. He lost all bearing on what he was doing. They lost elevation with a belly-afflicting drop. His canines erupted to their full length and piercing sharpness. But then an obstruction loomed out through the night, became a rooftop. Anso glanced off a chimney, caught the fall with bent legs, and halted there for a bit to get his bearings. Regain focus. Assemble his thoughts. And work at control. The entire time, the leather pants pinched his erection. Almost paining.

And he'd felt that, too!

Anso shoved his head back and sent a cry of absolute joy into the night about them. He couldn't halt it. This was too incredible! Unbelievably astonishing! And beyond wondrous.

He leapt back into the sky. Leah didn't react. There was no question as to why. He knew. She was under his thrall. He hadn't wanted to use his powers, but she'd left him little choice. What he'd been experiencing was beyond comprehension or containment. Now that he had her in his arms, the sensations went beyond that. They approached a level he could barely conceive. Or control.

And she wanted him to leave her?

Wait an entire day?

*Never.*

The tops of trees came into view. A rock face loomed from the mist-filled dark next. Anso flew upward along it. His heart racing. His pulse joining in.

And...finally!

He overshot the tower, skidded to a stop against the cliff face. A spin put his shoulder in position to take the brunt of landing. A scrape opened on his skin. He barely felt it. Everything was too attuned to one thing. The woman in his arms. His mate. His clumsiness had jostled her slightly. Anso pulled her close. Held her tight. She was the perfect heft in his arms. Solid. Womanly. He took a deep breath of her particular vanilla-imbued scent. He rocked in place. And silently cursed his clumsiness.

He might have hurt her.

And that would be unforgiveable.

Her head shifted. Fragrant hair brushed his chin. That small event sent a surge of lightning through him. Anso tightened his belly. Thighs. Arms. All, in an effort to control the scope of reaction. Curb unbelievable force. Tamp down desire and urge. Massive need. Everything on him was alerted. Primed. And desperate.

There wasn't any light source on the balcony. He could still see. Much too easily. She was so beautiful! Her eyes were large, light-colored, surrounded by soot-shaded eyelashes. Her incredibly plump, red-toned lips were pursed, as if begging a kiss. Her breath came in heaves, each one lifting and displaying a bosom that demanded attention. Anso glanced down. Jerked his gaze back up. Stifled any response with clenched teeth that sliced into his lower lip. He locked his muscles tighter next, sending tremors through them.

Despite his efforts, the groan slipped past his lips. He lowered his chin. Sought her gaze and locked to it. Concentrated. Sent mesmeric power in waves that were nearly visible. She regarded him for several long moments. Their hearts thumped in tandem. Each breath matched. And his shaking intensified until his boot heels clicked audibly against stone.

"Well. This is...unexpected."

*Unexpected?*

That was her word for this? He was dealing with a morass of emotion that threatened to unman him, and she was immune? What had happened to his enthralling powers? And then he knew. They needed light. He couldn't connect with her unless they locked gazes. And for that, she'd need to see him.

"We need light," she remarked, reading his mind.

"Yes."

Anso raced beneath a carved black stone arch that looked natural, reached a courtyard open to the elements. Crossed it. A moment later, they were at one of the heavy wooden doors that accessed his home. He was shaking as he entered a hall. Selected a chamber.

*Ah.*

He was in luck.

He'd reached the silver rooms.

These had just been cleaned. Aired. He had eight bedroom suites. Never used. Kept ready. Available.

Maintained if, and when, he remembered. The silver suite was perfect. This *must* be fate. Not only was it dust-free and immaculate, but these rooms were the most richly appointed. Black rock walls had been covered over with wall hangings of silk, interspersed with real silver threads. The rock floors were strewn with rugs of white and silver hue. The furniture was white ash, heavily embossed with more silver, while the linens were the finest silk. Ermine lined another treasure – a coverlet of the finest woven damask, also heavily embroidered with silver.

Anso smacked through the door, and flew through the receiving salon and into the bed chamber before he heard the sound of the door thudding shut. His movement turned on the motion-activated lighting. Candles started flickering from multiple candelabra, as if they were real and not the latest technology. The glow tempered the effect of so much silver, but the rooms still sparkled. Leah gasped. He felt, more than heard it as she lifted her head from him and viewed the enclosure.

He experienced what had to be a flash of pride. It added to the mix of emotions he was already suffering. Honed them. And why? Because his home wasn't antiquated. There was a river below the edifice with enough water flow to supply electricity. Indoor plumbing. A natural gas vent gave him everything else a human might require. It was all another mark that he'd foregone his barbarian roots.

"This is—." Her voice stopped. She shook her head.

"Yes?" Anso prompted.

"Not what I had in mind."

Her words had the effect of a splash of cold water. It chilled, sent a sizzling sound through his ears, but then it quickly dissipated. Anso straightened slightly. The move lifted her. He tried to keep a defensive tone from his reply. It probably failed. The words were also slurred around his fangs. Almost unintelligible.

"It's...not?"

"I was thinking more on the line of illuminating things so I could figure them out. I was not planning on going even deeper into psychosis."

"This is my silver chamber," he informed her.

"I'll buy that...but that. Right there. Is a bed."

"Yes."

Her essence drew him. He tightened his arms more. Lifted her easily. Lowered his nose to her ear. Found the perfect spot below it.

...the line of her throat.

"Anso."

She said his name with a voice that trembled. Anso inhaled. Held the breath for long moments. And then exhaled. It was stupid, akin to fanning a fire. Taking any banked spark and flashing it to life. But it was impossible to stop the mating force. He'd given up trying. She didn't understand. She was too necessary. Her essence too vital. Joining with her compulsory. Beyond containment.

*...and her blood!*

"You need...to put me down."

Her voice was a bare tremor of sound that ended in a low moan. Anso opened his mouth and licked a trail into existence along her throat, held his tongue at the lifted section of a vein as it throbbed with her pulse beat. And then he answered.

"No."

The word was whispered against her neck. He watched her skin lift with shivers. His canines responded instantly. With raging need. He licked his lips. Shuddered in place. Fought to control the uncontrollable. He wanted her desperately, but he wanted her just as willing. Hungry. Afire with the same inferno of desire he faced.

"If I wish...a man into existence...the least he can do...is obey."

*Wish?*

*Obey?*

Had she really linked those two words? Caught her breath several times through the sentence? And moaned the last word? And she expected him to make sense?

Anso grunted. He was losing his last restraint. The force he held back kept mounting. It was just as he'd said, what felt like eons ago at the steps. Where they'd met. She didn't understand.

"Did you really wish for a man tonight?"

"Um. Forget I just said that, okay?"

Her skin moved against his teeth, slicing the smallest bit. Anso lifted several inches from the floor. Hovered there as the first hint of her blood seeped to the surface. Slowly sank back down.

"Any...man? Or me?"

The words were harsh-sounding. Almost guttural. Easily demonstrating how they'd grated against his throat.

"Anso."

His name was a breathless tone, filled with emotion. He could only hope it was as it sounded – desperation.

"And you expect...obedience?"

The words were difficult to understand. He didn't have much time left to explain them, either. His fangs were throbbing. His rod pressed against leather in accompaniment. This was becoming torment...to a painful degree.

"Just kiss me already!"

Anso rocked in place. Groaned. And did something much more potent.

He bit her.

# CHAPTER FOUR

Leah had always dealt with things from a certain standpoint. She believed that the mind was in control. The way a person experienced life was due to how their brain processed the data it received. Mind power was the key. It controlled everything, even physical response. The mind was the all-powerful controlling factor.

But it could do some strange things.

It brought monsters to life and made them terrifying entities, sent unshakable dark clouds to darken a sunny day, altered a beauty queen's reflection into that of an ogre. The mind could turn any happy moment into a morass of decay and darkness. Most of her clients had contemplated suicide before seeing her. None had gone through with it.

And she was determined to keep that record.

That's why she'd become a psychologist. She had a real gift. She'd felt it since childhood. She could relate to a person while she met with them, figure out and empathize with their underlying issues, and work with them. She didn't conquer demons, she helped people figure out how to do it themselves. With that came a real sense of fulfillment and contentment. Leah had a lot of satisfied clients who referred her services to others. Steven commented on it at every monthly meeting.

She was absolutely certain the mind was the key to a happy life. It was able to see through any number of things to find reality. For some reason, hers had decided to take an unscheduled hiatus after the fourth shot of vodka, as if – all of a sudden –she'd developed an allergy to alcohol and this was a Substance-Induced Psychotic Disorder. Or, maybe somebody had slipped her a drug for some reason and she was suffering Substance-Induced     Psychotic     Disorder     with Hallucinations. Hard to believe Steven wouldn't have seen that.

Or – just maybe – this was easily explainable. Perhaps she'd fallen off the bench and hit her head, knocking herself unconscious. It was possible. Fairly improbable – but still, there had to be an explanation for this. Because facts were facts. Immutable. Absolute. Incorruptible.

This man – this almost god-like guy – did not exist. He couldn't. Not only was he way too gorgeous but he created all kinds of physical havoc throughout her body. Those were both impossible. Anso had not grabbed her to him and leapt into thin air. Nor had he somehow sped through the night sky. She'd watched it happen. That didn't make it real. As for this silver room? The one with the big bed and decadently luxurious bedding? It didn't exist, either, although if she had conjured up the perfect seductive atmosphere, she'd have imagined something like this.

Exactly.

Maybe she was just dreaming. It was very real, but some dreams were. And she had been tired. Perhaps the history of the city had gotten to her...as well as lack of sex. She could be suffering Hypoactive Sexual Disorder due to Separation Anxiety, but she doubted it. She'd had a good physical workout, sat down to rest, and this was the result. She'd gotten tired of waiting for the tour group, settled onto the bench, and simply nodded off. The chill hadn't been conducive to a nap, but that was the most probable explanation for this. Because anything else was really 'off-the-charts' unbelievable.

But then Anso did something to her neck, and everything she thought she knew got upended.

And then obliterated.

The most heavenly symphony of sensation shot through her. Everywhere. Her breasts immediately felt fuller, heavy, and extremely sensitive. Her belly got a tickling sensation just before heat slammed through it on the way to her loins. And with that plethora of fire came an itch of irritation, and a lot of carnal desire.

A lot.

A heavy throbbing sound started up in the room, pulling her pulse into rhythm with it. Loud. Deep. Continual. Without any instruction from her, she turned toward him, shoved her breasts into his chest and started moving. Sinuously matching the beat about her. Her nipples went to hard knots against the lace-cupped bra –which should have scratched at least some of the itch – but, it didn't. And the stupid silk blouse buttoned in the back. She couldn't get any closer despite how she desperately needed to. And worse. The frustration turned into a cry that she actually voiced.

*Oh no!*

She was acting like a female in heat, something that should be exactly as embarrassing as it sounded...except that Anso pulled away from her and sent a harsh, bestial sound into existence. It blended with the throbbing permeating the room, lifted shivers all over her body, and covered over any noise she made. He also began shuddering so violently it lifted them from the floor. And they didn't come back down.

"Bed," she said.

"Yes," he answered.

A moment later, her back, shoulders, and buttocks met the embroidered surface of that exquisite coverlet. Anso was right with her, holding her to him. Covering. Enclosing. His hands slid along her arms, he twined his fingers with hers, and swung his arms wide, pushing their conjoined hands above her head, and then he stopped. For an incalculable amount of time. Poised above her. Looking down at her. Their gazes locked. Their breaths became huge heaves for air. Commingling. Raising rivulets of shivers that each spewed sparks.

And there was something really strange about his mouth.

Those weren't—?

He had *fangs?*

Oh. No way. She had to dream up a gorgeous masculine god and then add in vampirism? Handsome, dark, and masculine weren't enough? She had to stir a dangerous vibe in with the sexual ones already shooting off him? She struggled briefly against him but the pleasure of his touch, his body against hers left her panting with want. Hungry with need.

"Ans—?"

The name wasn't finished. He tipped his head down, tickled the sides of her face with his unbound hair, and slammed his lips to hers. Leah sucked in air that brought a salty tang. She licked, and after the first taste, she was returning the kiss. Her body lurched up in surprise, the reaction mixed with pleasure, a torrent of unleashed passion. A tsunami of desire. Blizzard of want.

And a complete need for immediacy.

And then the kiss ended. Anso's weight disappeared. The man moved with incredible speed. He was a blur at the side of the bed. Leah watched him shuck his sword and a long dagger somewhere behind him. They clattered against the stone floor. The leather strapped about his shoulders got pulled off next; the matching cuffs were yanked off his wrists, and then he started on his belt. The entire time, he didn't move his eyes from hers.

*Well.*

She didn't need another hint. This was really happening. She might as well go with it. *Oh. Screw that idea.* She was going to be an active participant. It might be a dream, but it was the best damn dream she'd ever had. It would probably ruin her sex life for the rest of her mortal years. Turn her off every future encounter.

Leah ignored the slightest hint of inner voice.

The one that cautioned.

Warned.

And got silenced.

She sat, shoved her shoes off. Crawled to her knees, and—

*This was weird.*

It was her dream, yet she still wore Steve's coat. How was that possible? It was undamaged, too. Well. No way was she damaging it. Or wrinkling it. Or doing anything that might clue Steven into the fact that she'd had a sex dream to end all sex dreams. Not even Doctor Freud would be able to analyze this. Leah opened buttons. The coat fell off. There wasn't a hook in sight, so she did the next best thing. She stood and reached upward, barely managing to access the top of a cannonball post on the footboard so she could drape the suit coat over it.

Then she swiveled, looked over and then down to Anso. And her jaw dropped.

*Holy shit.*

The man hadn't been idle. He'd shed his clothing and stood staring up at her with eyes that glowed a strange shade. Dark red. Like pooled blood. But she didn't lock gazes with him this time. Nor did she stop and mentally process what really did look like fangs. There was a reason. Anso was a massive and chiseled male. She didn't have any way to avoid seeing and recognizing just how massive and chiseled. And he certainly wasn't suffering Male Erectile Dysfunction. *Oh. My.* He had his hands on his hips, his pose indicative of a Michelangelo sculpture. Only Anso had a lot more than any nude model she'd ever seen. He was obviously proud of that fact.

With good reason.

*Oh. My. My. My.*

She'd been right. This dream was going to ruin her for any other man. And any other interlude. For life. And...what the heck? It was going to be worth it!

But wait!

*Damn everything.*

She couldn't go through with this. The man standing before her deserved a supermodel for a lover, someone as fit as he was. Not a woman with a weight problem. One who wore goddess-sized clothing from specialty stores. Atop a girdle thing called shape-wear.

*Oh. Crap.*

She'd forgotten that. She'd have red marks. She'd probably look like a stuffed sausage. There was too much light in the room for this, and—

Anso growled.

He literally *growled*.

Bass tones surged through the room with such power it lifted strands of her hair. The notes reached out and joined the thumping rhythm already in existence. Her thighs trembled with a rush of weakness. Her knees were next. Leah grabbed onto the footboard post to keep from falling. She moved her glance to the wood. It was solid. Heavy. Cool to the touch. And even that felt erotic between her breasts!

"What?" she whispered.

"You need to finish. Now."

Leah cleared her throat. It sounded ineffectual, and proved as much when she spoke, trying to sound assertive, even while facing the post. "Whoa. Anso. Um. There is machismo, and there is over-the-top macho. And I'm telling you—."

"I warn you, *wiblih*. You do not have much time."

She gasped. Her eyes went wide. Her voice managed to work. "What...does that word mean?"

"Female."

Her eyes went even wider.

"I will tear your clothing from you."

*He wouldn't dare.*

She sent a glance toward him. He looked like it wasn't an idle threat. And damn everything. He also looked amazing masculine, supremely turned on, and even more defined and large than before.

Everywhere.

*Well.*

*What the hell.*

This was her dream, but if this fantasy-god made one wisecrack about her Junoesque figure or love handles or how she needed to hit a gym or stay away from the doughnuts – just one – she was ending this. She only hoped she didn't cry for a week afterward, too.

The linen jacket came off easily. The blouse buttons at the back of her neck gave her a little trouble. She pulled the silk over her head, creating static that lifted hair strands with the motion. Now that her jacket was off, the tight confines of her skirt were on display. She had to peel it down over her hips before shimmying it to a pool of fabric at her ankles. She glanced down. She'd been right. The flesh-toned girdle made her look like a stuffed sausage. She should have bought the larger size. She braved a glance toward Anso to see his reaction. He was frowning. His upper lip was lifted in a sneer. And there was no denying it.

He really did have fangs. *Real ones!*

*Oh, shit.*

*Oh, shit*

*Oh, shit.*

"You are a maid?" he asked.

Leah blinked. She had to process this. Her mind needed to—

"Is that why you wear a chastity belt?" he continued.

"A...what?"

"That."

He pointed. At her girdle. Leah blushed severely. A portion of her brain told her this was not how a dream was supposed to go. The rest of her was beyond thought. Her entire body was alert. Despite embarrassment, she felt irritated. Moist. Ready.

She knew exactly what she wanted.

And where.

She licked her lips. "There is nothing chaste...about this, okay? It's a foundation garment. For a full-figured woman."

Anso growled again, this time in an even lower timbre, as if that was even possible. The throbs of sound about her went louder. Stronger. And the same exact sequence of events happened throughout her body, only this time the weak feeling wasn't just at her legs. It slithered a bit higher and that messed with her ability to think, speak, and breathe.

"N-now what?" she asked.

"I grant you time to explain."

She pulled in a long breath to answer. It sounded like a gasp to her ears. And – *damn everything* – she even stuttered. "L—l-look. Um. A-Anso? I—. This is not a chastity belt. Okay? I'm not a virgin. This is a girdle. I'm wearing it to create...um. Womanly curves! You know. To make me look...thinner."

Her voice fell off. It was his fault. His frown deepened, and now he looked angry. Almost scary. And those fangs of his were white. Long. Sharp. Impossible to miss. And incredibly sexy. He breathed in huge gulps of air as he glared up at her, and exhaled them just as harshly. She watched his eyes roam the length of her body. Back to her face. Her heart sank. He was going to deny her, laugh at her, turn away...

Then the expression in them changed, softened, warmed as he looked upon her.

"You are *sconi! Wein.* A *gimma.* Your taste is so *suozi!* Sweeter than *honag.* You are beyond perfect! You hear me? Your *brust* are—! And your *arsebelli is*—! You are the epitome of *gisunt!*"

"Wh-what does...all that mean?"

Her whisper barely made sound. He tossed back his head and yelled something completely unintelligible. The view was unbelievable. His chest darkened. Striations welted across pecs. Upper arms. Abs. Veins lifted in his throat. Several things throughout the room rattled, and some of the lighting disappeared as if candles were blown out. And the throbbing sounds got even louder, swelling in accompaniment to his voice. Depth. And intensity.

He lowered his head. The hungered look he gave her stole her breath. Took her wits. Scrambled her innards.

And then his body slammed against hers.

"You were warned, *wiblih*."

# CHAPTER FIVE

Anso should have used English, but he'd felt such a spark of anger at her reasons for wearing such a garment, followed by a flood of warmth as he realized she meant them, that it nonplussed and confused. He'd reverted to ancient Germanic words she wouldn't even understand. He'd explain later. Right now, he had a goddess in his arms, a bed at his feet, and a heated, heavy, almost painful problem at his groin.

He'd used incomprehensible words, but it was the best he could manage. She dared denigrate her beauty? Her softness? Her womanly form? He would never understand women! She'd have been the favorite in any king's harem, including his.

He only wished he had the right words, the words from his heart, to tell her!

His mate's taste was sweet, true, but far sweeter than any honey. She was a vision of the perfect *wiblih*. Her hair was a dark brown shade, interspersed with strands that carried a magenta tone...like that of dried blood. Her eyes were a clear, light green. They fascinated. Intrigued. Entranced. He could get lost in her gaze. No wonder his enthralling power didn't work with her. He was powerless against such beauty. Gazing into Leah's eyes was an experience of wonder, as if he'd found the gateway to everything he'd lost. It was pure *zoubar* – magic. She gave him back *liben* – life. *Lioban* – love. And he mustn't forget. He had physical prowess back! He had the ability to *semantwist* again! His *gimaht* stood hard and proud and extended for her – because of her.

She truly didn't understand.

She was everything to him.

She called herself full-figured? Wore some tortuous-looking garment to create womanly curves? The woman needed better mirrors. She was a goddess! The image of health and beauty! Her body was that of his dreams. She had a lace band about her *brust* that didn't do a thing to cover them. Her breasts were full. Large. Topped with little rosy nipples the lace didn't hide. That bosom of hers demanded more than a look. His mouth had actually watered. And that was before he factored in her thighs!

The woman was crazed.

His mate was lush. Entirely womanly. The garment she wore didn't detract from a view of thighs so amply curved, perfectly rounded, and deliciously firm, he longed to drop to her feet and *beton*. That is what a man did when gifted with such a banquet of perfection.

He worshipped it.

Anso held her against him with one arm, pressing her softness close despite how it mangled his effort at self-control and sent massive ache through his groin. He shook as he yanked the embroidered coverlet from the bed, revealing sheets of pristine silver-shaded silk. Suffered a succession of tremors as he placed her reverently atop the sheets, looked at her perfect body for another moment...fought the urge to crush himself against her again.

And lost.

With a groan Anso launched atop her, wrapped his arms about her, and rolled, pulling her atop him, so that he could shove the lacy contraption off of her bosom, revealing exactly the perfection he expected to find. And lose his mind.

He delved into absolute heaven. Seized and held her breasts together so he could suckle both nipples into hard darts capable of piercing his tongue. The entire time Leah writhed atop him, tormenting him further with each wiggle she made against him. Every push. Each touch. He'd been off a bit. This wasn't *zoubar*. Magic was too small a word. Her soft feminine cries added all kinds of sensations to the experience and Anso pulled back in order to voice his own cry of pleasure, only his sounded like a howl. Her thighs tightened about him and she moved, sliding into position to straddle his rod. A greater fire joined the almost-torturous pressure of her garment against him.

Her undergarments were the enemy.

And this was war.

Anso grabbed the lace center of her bra and ripped it apart. The entire thing sprang back to dangle from her arms as if catapulted. And then he was working at her foundation thing. But the more he pulled, the more it flexed and fought him. His efforts made the bed sway and rock. Her breasts moved in accompaniment. Anso shoved his head back into the mattress, and this time, his howl was distinct for what it was – absolute and complete frustration.

"It's...spandex," she whispered.

"No. It's *hella*." He answered back, his voice a croak of sound. "And you are never wearing it again! Ever!"

"Says...who?"

"Me!"

The word reverberated through the chamber with the force he spoke it. All sorts of things rattled. Something fell with a crash. More of the fake candles fell from their perches, some going dim and extinguishing. Some came to rest on the floor, illuminating from there.

"I...think I...can get...it off."

She dropped to his chest, smashing her glorious breasts against him. Anso didn't control the jerk of reaction as he pulsed upward. She didn't seem to notice. She had her cheek against his, her shoulders aligned with his, and her thumbs hooked beneath the garment edge. All so she could start peeling at it. The entire time she wriggled, bumping countless times against his erection, sending electrically charged stimuli each time that touched. Teased. And tormented to a level he'd never experienced.

Anso tightened every muscle. Sent the command. His canines weren't the lone thing a vampire wielded. His fingernails grew. Became knife-sharp. Razor-honed. He half sat, unable to lift far without moving her, and then he pushed her hands aside to shove his beneath the garment. The material resisted momentarily, but failed to stop him. Within moments, he'd stuck his nails through and then he ripped downward, peeling the damn thing open down both sides.

Leah gasped. And then she was helping. Every move releasing more of her to his hands. Succor. Wonder. He concentrated to retract his nails, and his rod found her center. She was wet. Incredibly hot. At his touch, she stiffened and keened the most beautiful sound into existence. Anso went wild.

He spun, placing her on her back beneath him before her cry finished, and started pushing at her core. Her thighs enwrapped him, helping him. She was so tight. So incredibly hot. So lusciously firm. Her small cries accompanied each push. Every inch gained. Moist coils of tension gripped tightly to him, assisting and yet threatening. Anso almost lost his ability to pleasure her, as well. He tightened everything. Fought the distinct pressure already in place at his center. Grunted with the effort. Denied the instinct to thrust, and keep thrusting. Held back the urge for fulfillment. Shook with the effort. The entire bed rattled in accompaniment. She was so soft. So womanly. So welcoming. And at the same time, so tight he was actually afraid of hurting her.

"Anso—!"

His name on her lips held a hint of ire. Impatience.

"My *lioban*."

The word was hissed through a jaw so taut, his canines grazed his chin, slicing skin. Opening cuts. He weakened slightly. Gave another push. Another.

And was finally there.

Deep within her.

Sheathed by a moist paradise of indescribable dimension. It enveloped. Caressed. Stimulated. Anso called on every bit of strength he possessed to stay immobile as she absorbed his size, holding back when everything on him demanded the opposite. Somehow restrain urges that hovered at the periphery of every moment that passed. A sob escaped him.

And Leah moved.

Her thighs tightened about him and she pushed, shoving down into the mattress, sliding a bit from him. At her return Anso grabbed fistfuls of bedding, shredding the silk. All for an anchor so he could thrust, and there was no stopping this time. She was too perfect. The sensations too viciously delicious. He pumped, thrusting his entire length into her. And back out. Again. And again. Over and over. His movements grew wilder. Fuller. Pushing him seemingly endless amounts deeper. More. Again. And the entire time, she matched his rhythm with words that thrilled. Encouraged.

And ignited.

"Oh. Oh. Anso! Oh. Oh!"

Power filled his veins. Force propelled his moves. The mattress jumped in cadence. The bedposts creaked in accompaniment. Matching his every push. Each move back. The return thrust. Over and over. Each one going deeper. A sob caught at the back of his throat. He swallowed it back, yanked the bedding down to gain more solidity so he could push even harder. Stronger. Faster.

Leah screamed.

And Anso exploded.

His mouth opened. He roared. The sides of his mouth split with the depth and volume of it. The force of his release propelled them upward. Well above the bed. Leah's legs clenched tightly to him while he had his arms wrapped about her, clutching her close as his body pulsed through wave after wave of the purest pleasure. It was beyond scope. Nearly impossible to imagine. Perfect bliss snatched at him. Grabbed tightly. And then claimed ownership. Every prior experience he'd ever had in *semantwist* got annihilated. Blasted into oblivion. And overwritten by something that sent a stab of tears to his eyes.

Mating had been described in basic words to him. This act of love had been mentioned. There hadn't been anything said about how deep the feeling would be when it hit. Nor how beautiful. She was watching him as the pleasure started ebbing. Any power he claimed started evaporating. With very little warning. There was a gloss of moisture atop her eyes, illumining them into green-shaded pools of mystery. She smiled. His heart gave an almost painful surge. He didn't move. He didn't dare.

A shadow of something that could be doubt crossed her features. He wouldn't allow that. Anso returned her smile. He should have waited. That simple gesture drained the last vestige of his strength. They dropped. He spun just before they landed, taking the brunt of it on his back. The mattress jounced with their arrival before resettling.

And that's when he started laughing.

# CHAPTER SIX

Something was seriously wrong here.

She hadn't awakened.

Leah wasn't thinking of being jolted to awareness by an alarm, or a phone, or some other outside interference. The dimensions of this fantasy should have triggered wakefulness. Dreams were not this vivid. Not hers, anyway. She'd never encountered anything like this. The pleasure hadn't just been orgasmic. That might have been in an acceptable range. No. What she'd just experienced was earth-shattering. Foundation-shaking. Almost scary.

This couldn't be a dream. It really might be a drop off the cliff of sanity. And sooner or later, even hallucinations had to end. Reality was going to intrude. That was going to hurt. She wondered if there was some way to mute this dreamscape down any. Keep it from being so damn big.

What a misnomer.

She wasn't just dreaming big here.

This was over-the-top enormous.

This vision was one for the record books. Of course, she'd have to tell someone about it first.

*Oh!* What an impossible concept! How could she describe the most gorgeous guy she'd ever seen? That was already huge. She needed better words, but couldn't think of any at the moment. He was beyond handsome. Built. Perfectly formed. And he knew exactly how to use it. Everything about Anso was large. And that laugh of his! *Holy crap.* The guy had a deep booming laugh that sent echoes through the rooms as it faded. Big didn't even begin to describe the enormous bed that had just materialized for her either, nor a mattress up to the challenge of some really big lovemaking moves...with a lot of thrust and power behind them. She hadn't even factored in the weight. She mustn't forget that. She wasn't a stick-thin woman, but Anso was beyond heavy. The guy rocked some solid muscle. That equaled a lot of poundage. Even now, he dented the mattress so that her body stayed suctioned to him – not that she'd have moved.

Perish that idea! Move? No way. She'd never felt more cherished. More desired. More beautiful. Nor more womanly.

Ever.

Too bad it was all in her mind.

She must have felt more emotion over her break-up than she'd thought. Stuffed it deep into her psyche where even she didn't notice. And, while it was bad timing, it was possible. Deep-seated emotional trauma could trigger Generalized Anxiety Disorder that could be followed with a Delusional Disorder. That diagnosis might fit her predicament. Only this delusion wasn't frightening or sinister, like some of her patients had described to her during therapy sessions. Leah was living her very own perfect private paradise. And that's when she made her decision. It might be a mistake, but if this was just a Brief Psychotic Disorder, she was staying in it as long as possible. The psychologists at the convention could all take a flying leap off the historic Charles Bridge.

One-at-a-time.

Steven included.

That thought raised a chuckle. Leah stifled it with a swallow before it made sound, in case that altered anything. Everything was too incredibly wonderful. She probably glowed. She had to get everything committed to memory. Locked away. Safe. Secure. Secret. It was her possession. To pull up and savor whenever she liked...and especially when life grew especially lonely and bleak. She mustn't stop at the things she could see, touch, and smell, either. *Oh. Hell no.* There was a whole level of things happening here. Emotions. Passions. A treasure-trove of sensations. Beyond huge. They'd been *gigantic*. Unbelievably intense. And absolutely incredible.

She didn't even dare open her eyes. She'd had them shut since Anso fell onto the bed. She hadn't looked when they'd dropped back down. She didn't have to see where she was or guess what position. Anso had his arms locked about her, holding her to him. They were even still joined. His body occasionally suffered a tremor. Each time, the area around her heart warmed rapidly and markedly. As if she felt something beyond lust for him.

*Uh oh.*

That idea was even more fantasy she didn't want to analyze. Not until later. Much. Much. Later.

"*Lioban?*"

Her man was calling.

Leah opened her mouth to answer and then shut it. What in the heck? *Her man?* She did not just think that. Oh no. No. No way. Not her. Leah was a confident, self-employed, highly sought after psychologist. She didn't have any Gender Disorder Issues. On any level. And she wasn't allowing any man to upend—

"Leah."

Breath touched her forehead. His arms tightened. Her heart pulsed almost painfully within her breast. All signs of real trouble. She *did not* feel anything for him! She didn't. She couldn't. She refused. They'd just met. Had fantastic sex. And—

"I know you can hear me."

Leah sighed and opened her eyes. Looked up. Her heart gave another solid thump. A lock of dark sable-colored hair had fallen forward, sending a shadow to his nose. Light sent a glint to each eye, visible as he blinked. She didn't know their exact color. They were really dark. Mysterious. Deep. But it was the look on his face that stole her breath. She'd never seen such an expression.

Now, she knew how it felt to be adored, too.

He smiled. His expression softened even more. He had little lines at the sides of his eyes, lengthy ones in both cheeks – both signs that he smiled often. He wasn't clean-shaven, but the scuff of whiskers added a rakish edge to his persona that he really didn't need. The man was beyond gorgeous. He was absolute male beauty that had been given a physical form. Despite that, he didn't seem to have any vestige of Narcissistic Personality Disorder, and he was the perfect candidate for that diagnosis. Not once had he preened or flexed, or even checked for his reflection in a mirror. And this incredibly gorgeous man was with her. She almost shook her head. It was as incredible as it was unbelievable.

"You are all right? I did not hurt you?"

"What?" Leah blinked several times with the surprise. The man had given her perfection. She might be tender, but it was a delicious feeling. She wouldn't trade it for anything. He grunted.

"I am a large man. And you are a very small *wiblih.*"

Leah snorted. His smile faded slightly, while his brows drew down.

"You laugh at me?"

"No. I just—. It's just—. Um. Men have called me a lot of things...over the years. Small...is not one of them," Leah whispered.

He glanced down to where her breasts were smashed against him. His entire body shuddered, shaking hers with it. He had it conquered before he returned his gaze to hers. Leah's heart smacked into her throat with a hard pulse that choked before it subsided.

*Oh no.*

*No.*

This reaction was not because she was falling for him. No way. Not her. It was because he was so handsome that looking at him was difficult. That had to be the reason. He licked his lips. She glanced to his mouth. There wasn't a hint of fangs.

*Good.*

"Parts of you are not," he finally replied.

Leah returned her attention to his eyes. He'd turned his head, which put the light fully onto his face. Her heart did another heave. Only this time, it landed in her belly and decided to pound from there.

She swallowed.

Tried ignoring it.

Failed.

"Parts of you are so tiny, I worry," he continued. "While others? Ah! I cannot think! There are no words good enough! Your *brust* is...full. Womanly. Very soft. While your *huf and arsebelli—!"*

He twinged deeply within her, hard again. Easily as erect as before. Leah's body instantly responded without one instruction from her. She squeezed about him. And then she did it again. Anso groaned, and this time his shuddering rocked the bed.

"You must not do that, *lioban.*"

Leah licked her lips. Thought for a moment. Decided to try a deflecting question. Maybe that would work at calming things.

"Um. This word *brust.* Is that breast?"

He sent a breath onto her before nodding.

"And *arsebelli* would be...?"

She left it open-ended. He supplied the word through what sounded like clenched teeth.

"Buttocks."

"And *lioban?*"

Her body wasn't following a thing she requested. If anything, her movements about him got tighter while her squeezing had become continual surges that didn't obey the slightest command.

"Please! You do not understand! It is too soon!"

A sound suspiciously like a sob escaped his lips. But that couldn't be, because his voice had been harsh. Guttural.

"What does...*lioban* mean?"

She tried deflection again. Even to her own ears she sounded strange. Breathless. Passionate. As if she suffered Hypoactive Sexual Desire Disorder or something with as much magnitude. A sex siren had taken over her throat and was issuing all kinds of signals, none of them calming. Anso closed his eyes. A look of agony crept across his features. And when he reopened them, the irises weren't dark anymore. They glowed red. Leah's eyes widened as they locked gazes.

"I warn you, *lioban*. We mustn't continue this. You must stop."

He could say it. She might try to obey. Her body had an entirely different agenda, however.

"I don't know how," she told him.

He pushed up, shoved his head back, and yelled something that didn't have words to it. And then he dropped his head and glared down at her. His upper lip was lifted. Definite fang tips were erupting from his canine teeth. They grew long and sharp as she watched. She should have been shocked and horrified. She wasn't. The emotions were much closer to fascination. A scientific-based interest, overridden by complete allure.

"You are my *weibchan*, Leah. I am powerless against this. You must stop me. It is too...soon!"

"You have fangs," she told him.

"Everything on me demands that we...join again! And...again! And as many times...as we can!"

He punctuated each sentence with a thrust into her, adding bass tones to the room. Each one carried emotion. She recognized some of it because it matched hers. Desperation. Anger. Need. Alarm bells got silenced in her mind. Her breath grew quicker. Harsher. She matched each inhalation he made, and every exhalation. Exactly. Her heart thudded in heavy beats that had a loud echo, as if his heart was in sync. Her belly warmed. Grew hot. Flames sparked to life within her. They licked at her skin, singeing her lower belly, upper thighs. And then they ignited an inferno at her core.

Leah gripped her legs about him, lifted her hips, and shoved, forcing him deeper within her.

Anso responded with a snarl and a series of thrusts that sent her head toward the headboard. He opened his mouth wide. This time she didn't have to wonder what he did to her throat. She knew. She watched him close in, felt the twin pricks as his fangs bit into her, followed by pulses of ecstasy that raced from the spot. The sensations smacked into erogenous zones she didn't know she possessed. Lighting more fires. Creating more craven needs. She greedily accepted each and every one. Actively participated.

And thoroughly enjoyed.

# CHAPTER SEVEN

*Good.*

His mate still slept. She hadn't awakened while he'd been gone and worried, wondering over his absence. She wouldn't know he'd donned trousers to forage through his kitchens, pillaging for anything she might find edible. He'd tried both pantries. Failed both times. He'd settled on bringing her a carafe of cold water. It probably wasn't enough, and she'd think it tasted horrible. He'd look farther afield once night fell again. He knew what she needed - nourishment. He also knew she couldn't get it from him.

Not for some time.

It had been too close already.

He watched Leah for long moments, inhaling each breath in tandem with her. Exhaling them with the same nuance. His heart continually beat within his chest, keeping rhythm with hers. She was on her side, curled up into a small section of the mattress, barely denting the surface. A hand pillowed her cheek.

He was so favored by the gods!

None other could have created such an exquisite female! She had a mass of dark brown hair that carried magenta streaks. Her eyelashes were even darker.

Thick. Lush. They contrasted vividly against her skin. She'd have looked cherubic, except her cheeks weren't rosy, her lips carried the barest hint of pink, and the rest of her portrayed a distinct pallor. It was especially noticeable against what was left of the silver-shaded bedding.

The sheets had been shredded on both sides of Leah. Long rents were the result of where he'd gripped at the mattress. The pillows had also been casualties. They'd been flung aside. One had burst open, showering the floor with feathers. The exquisite embroidered comforter had been another victim of their passion. It rested in a heap on the floor, the silver threads sparkling whenever candlelight hit them.

He hadn't changed her.

He still didn't know how he'd managed it.

Her blood was the purest bliss to him. Taking all of it had been a commanding need, reaching the highest physical level he'd ever experienced. He'd come very close to draining her, which was bad enough. Worse, was the fact that he hadn't replenished it with any of his fluid. Despite how every cell on his body had hated him, he'd pulled from her neck at the last possible moment, while she'd writhed and screamed and shuddered. He'd thrilled to every sign of fulfillment she'd given, while the entire time, he'd held back his own.

It had been the most supreme act of will Anso had ever exerted.

He approached the bed now with light steps, although she didn't stir. He didn't know how long she'd be in a semi-comatose condition. There wasn't anyone he could ask without incriminating himself. Anso had always been a leader. He wasn't born a king. He'd earned the position. And his kingdom had rules. Laws. Regulations. Without them, there was chaos. As king, he'd issued decrees. Enforced edicts. Exacted justice for transgressing. And he hadn't spared anyone.

But now that he'd broken a rule, he didn't know what to do. For the first time in his existence, he felt unsure. And that was a very bad place to be for a warlord.

Akron, the leader of the Vampire Assassin League would be livid. The rules were there for a reason; inviolate, except under the direst of circumstances. Life blood was not to be drained and replaced with vampiric fluid. No mate was to be changed unless they desired it...and knew the consequences beforehand.

That wasn't why Anso had pulled back, however.

He'd done it because Leah was perfect. And he wanted everything about her to be the same.

Anso ran a finger along her cheek, barely touching before he pulled away. Her lips trembled for a moment and then stilled. *Thank the gods.* She was warmer than the last time he'd checked. He stood, looked toward the ceiling of his chamber, and sent a heavy sigh of relief into the cavernous space.

He hadn't known relief was a tangible entity. He knew it now.

"An...so?"

His name was the vaguest whisper. He spun and dropped to a knee, placing him close to her level. "My *lioban?*"

She frowned slightly. Narrowed her eyes. "I'm still here."

She wasn't questioning it. He answered it anyway. "Yes."

"And...you're still here."

"Yes."

"That's...worrisome."

"You expected me to leave you?" he asked.

Her frown disappeared. "No. No. It's not that. It's—
." She stopped. Licked her lips. Trembled. "I'm...really
cold."

He snatched the coverlet from the floor and shook it
slightly before settling the soft underside of fabric onto
her, tucking it along her form. The material skimmed
her body. And then he had to choke back an instant
pinch of desire. It was unbidden. And intense. His rod
stirred against the leather pants, instantly interested. He
tightened his gut and held it.

"This is a beautiful comforter."

"Yes."

"Where did you get it?"

"I think France. Fourteenth century."

She jerked slightly. "Fourteenth century?"

"Perhaps fifteenth. I forget."

He shrugged, loosening his grip on his body. And
then he had to push back a rush of longing that had a
physical presence. He'd been accurate when describing
how mating felt with her earlier. Despite what might
happen, his body craved what only she could give.
Again. And again. And as many times as he could.

"You should use something a little less...costly."

"No."

She frowned. He scooted closer, scraping his knee
on the stone floor. That gained a slight impression of
hurt. He could feel such things as minor ache, too? The
timing was fortuitous. He used the pain as another bar,
caging a sense of yearning that just kept building.

"Maybe you could elaborate?" she said.

"What?" He was dealing with a plethora of physical needs and wants and cravings. He didn't dare voice any of them.

"You're wrapping me in a priceless antiquity here."

He glanced to the coverlet. Back to her face. "Oh. That."

"Yes. That. Why would you do such a thing? Perhaps the better question is, why on earth would I envision it?"

"It is the lone thing I have...at the moment...worthy of touching you."

She looked at him with astonishment for a moment. And then she answered. "Um. Wow."

"Perhaps it is you...who should elaborate," he requested.

"Oh. Funny. Funny. Ha. Ha," she replied.

Anso swallowed. Forced his mind to function. He still didn't comprehend her meaning. Or tone. He shook his head. "I do not understand."

"You don't?"

"No."

"That figures."

"Is the coverlet not to your satisfaction? I can fetch others."

"You have more of these?"

"Yes."

"Oh, why do I bother asking?"

Anso puzzled her words while she watched him with an unblinking gaze. His heart stuttered, or something equally noticeable. Hers did the same thing. She gasped, her eyes widened, and he nearly bolted onto the mattress to join her. Her struggle to sit stopped him. She was so weak! He was with her, a mass of still-intact pillows in his hand before she had a chance to collapse back down. She didn't say anything as he lifted her to the headboard, propped the pillows behind her, and resettled the coverlet about her. That was so stupid.

She was *too womanly*.

The yearning wasn't going away. He trembled more than once, and hoped she wouldn't note it, or decipher the cause.

The gods must be laughing at his predicament.

Anso sat on the edge of the mattress, rocking it slightly.

"I feel really...weird," she informed him.

"You do?"

"I feel fantastic, and yet, I'm really tired. I mean, look at me. I'm gasping for breath with just this small move. How is that possible? I feel like I've had the flu for a month."

He couldn't answer. He hadn't heard much past the request to look at her. She'd requested the one thing he was trying to avoid. Anso pulled more muscles tight. His canines tingled.

"I'm really thirsty," she told him.

"Oh. Yes. I brought water."

He leapt down, grabbed the carafe from the floor and returned. The mattress bounced with his arrival. She was watching him with a wide eyed expression again.

"You move...really fast. You know that?"

"Yes."

"I'm afraid to ask why."

"I am afraid of answering," he admitted.

She blinked several times. He watched with bated breath, a heart that was hitting his ribcage with painful beats, and a body that wouldn't obey his slightest command. His rod was pulsing against his trousers with movements she couldn't fail to see should she look, while his fangs had reached his lower lip. They were going to be noticeable. And soon.

"You? Afraid?"

"I am just as surprised as you are," he told her.

She laughed. The sound was sweet. Full. And created havoc through his torso. Anso yanked every muscle taut, leaning forward with the effort. Somehow, he got the craving shoved into submission, but it pounded against his restraint, letting him know it wasn't going to stay there.

"You are really cute. You know that?"

"What?"

"Does that...embarrass you?"

"Uh..."

"Crap. It figures. I suppose I should just drink some water, and shut up while I'm ahead. Right?"

He watched the silver threads sparkle as she moved. Felt the stab of his canines into his lower lip. Shook. The bed moved in accompaniment. And then he heard her gulps, followed by a sound suspiciously like she gagged. He glanced up. She had a horrified look on her face.

"Where did you get this water? The bottom of a sewer?"

"Forgive me," he replied.

Her eyes went shocked. "You *did*?"

"No." He shook his head.

"It tastes like—I can't even being to tell you how awful. Are you sure this is water?" She poured a few drops onto her hand. Looked at in the candlelight. "Looks clean."

"It is. I drew it myself from the well."

"You need to talk to somebody about your water system then, because this has to be the worst tasting water on the planet."

"It is not the water, *lioban*."

"Really? What is it then?"

"It is your tastes that have changed."

"This is getting nonsensical, Anso. Like...I've dropped down a rabbit hole or something equally impossible."

"This is not a rabbit hole. And you did not drop. I brought you here."

"Yeah. I know. We flew. I was there. Remember? You know, I really didn't want to analyze anything yet, but I suppose you're going to make me, aren't you?"

"What?"

"I've tried convincing myself I'm in a dreamscape here, but that's starting to wear thin. I don't even believe it anymore."

"You are not dreaming."

"Well...it was just a hope, because the other option is pretty bleak."

"Is it truly so bad?"

"I'm having a major psychotic episode, Anso. Okay?"

He frowned. "A what?"

"The mind conjures up some pretty heavy stuff sometimes. It's in the realm of Psychotic Disorder...and we might as well add in accompanying hallucinations, too."

His frown deepened. He lowered his chin. "I am confused, my *lioban.*"

"I'm a clinical psychologist, Anso. Do you know what that is?"

"No."

"I diagnose and treat unseen injuries and illnesses. Those that afflict the mind. I'm really good at figuring out what triggers psychotic episodes in others. I've never suffered one. Maybe that's it. I needed to know what my patients were going through so I could empathize more."

"Oh. You are not suffering anything like that, my *lioban.*"

"I don't even know what that word means."

"It means love," he answered.

She whistled. "Oh. Man. I have really gone over-the-top now. Shot right past Jupiter. I'm on my way to Neptune! You've been calling me love? Your love? This entire time?"

He nodded.

"And that's not psychotic to you?"

"Why would it be?"

"Oh, come on, Anso. You're a god among men. You know it. You even told me that's what your name means! And. Well. Let's just face it. I might be cute, but I'm a fat chick. Level with me, here."

Anger flooded his veins, adding fuel to an already massive fire. He found it difficult not to snarl. "By *hella!* What is it with you, woman? You are perfection! I have never beheld such beauty! You are never to call yourself that again! You hear me, *wiblih*? Ever! I will not allow it!"

"*You* won't allow it?

"No!"

"What on earth makes you think you have a say?"

He yelled the answer. Sound reverberated through the room, rattling fake candelabra, spilling several more of them. Lighting flickered and dimmed further. Leah gasped. He knew because he matched it. Anso moved onto his hands and knees. Approached where she was propped against the headboard.

"L-l-look. Anso? Um. My last boyfriend was just an asshole, and this...is getting a bit deep. I'll figure out the triggering event sooner or later, and then...well. It's going to be a hell of a memory for my old age. And...it isn't like I couldn't fall for you. Okay? Really fall. Far. And hard. If – of course – you were real. But nobody falls in love...at first sight. It's a romance trope. Okay?"

He lifted his upper lip, releasing his canines. He'd sliced skin. He could feel blood droplets as they hit his chin.

"Oh. No. No. Come on. Give me a break. You're already major sexy, Anso. But...um. Fangs? You have to actually have fangs?"

"Yes."

"Well. We're just going to have to talk about that now, too, aren't we?"

"Why?"

"Why? Because you have fangs!"

"Of course I have them. I am a vampire," Anso told her.

"Oh, no. No. Please? Can't you be something original? Like...a Succubus?"

"There is no such thing."

"There is no such thing as a vampire, either."

"You say that when you are with one?"

"Just because...you can grow fangs...doesn't mean anything. Okay? It means you're suffering...um. It's commonly known as Renfield's Syndrome. But that's just...a manifestation of Schizophrenia. It's not...real."

She had distinct pauses throughout the words. Her eyelids dropped slightly. Her lips parted. Sweet breath touched him. The bed was vibrating with a series of tremors that didn't just come from him.

"Le...ah."

He pulled the name from his depths. Bass tones resounded through the chamber. Her voice was a breathless hint of sound when she answered.

"Man. Oh, man. Do I...have the best imagination...in the world...or what?"

Her head fell back; displaying the purplish spots hadn't healed from where he'd punctured her throat before. They throbbed ever so slightly with her pulse. Anso studied them for a span. And then he pressed his mouth to hers.

And let her take this time.

# CHAPTER EIGHT

*I'm still here?*

What did that make it? A day? Two? A week? It was impossible to tell time. There didn't seem to be any windows.

Leah lifted her head from the mattress, and viewed the carnage of what had been pristine silken sheets. She focused on the ermine-trimmed, embroidered damask coverlet for a moment. It didn't look to have sustained any damage – any further damage anyway – and nothing of an irreparable nature. Either way, it shouldn't matter. This was just a Psychotic Delirium, but she still felt a sense of relief to know they hadn't ruined a priceless piece of medieval art, even if it was all in her head.

She looked out farther, taking in the room. Most of the candles were on the floor, in various stages of illumination. She could see now that they weren't real. There were little LED lights in their centers, some were still flickering. It was dim, but that didn't hamper her vision. She could easily see. A lot. And with perfect precision. As if she viewed things through telescopic lenses that adjusted at her whim. She'd been right. There weren't any windows. A lot of material covered the walls, in lengths of unbroken silver. It was echoed in the furniture. She picked out a chaise lounge chair. Two sofas. A loveseat. White wooden tables accented the setting. It looked elegant. Cold and aloof. As if it awaited the presence of a king.

Like Anso.

She didn't have to guess where he was. His weight compressed the mattress, making a well in the midst of the bed. She'd been sucked into it. She'd have a hard time moving away. She had her back to him, spooned in place, while one of his legs and an arm wrapped about her, as if making certain of her proximity.

This was so crazy. Nice, but crazy. She'd really like to stay here. Enjoy it. But that depended on the man holding her so tightly. And how reasonable he was willing to be. She didn't know if he was sleeping. He didn't snore. He didn't make any sound at all. She decided to test it.

"Anso?"

"Yes?"

The instant reply answered that question. He wasn't sleeping.

Leah rolled onto her back. His arms flexed to allow it. She looked up at him. Her heart dropped. Her breath caught. Her throat closed off. All physiological omens of something bad. She'd been afraid Anso would ruin her sex life with a real male in the real world. Falling in love with him would be beyond stupid. That was bound to give her a Dissociative Disorder. She'd need pharmaceutical treatment. Years of therapy. She'd have to quit her practice. Sell her condo. Change her phone number. Cancel her social networking accounts...

"You are very beautiful this morning."

*Shit.*

Her heart reacted with a thud that lodged it in her throat. Or something as powerful. It hurt to swallow.

"How do you know it's morning?" she asked.

He smiled. "Instinct. Preservation. Experience."

"You could just put in windows."

"Sunlight is not a good idea."

"Really? Why not?"

"Vampires—"

She interrupted him. "Don't do the vampirism thing again, Anso? Please? I feel too good. It's too soon. We can make it a ground rule. No mention of vampires. Or blood-letting. Or Succubus. Or...mental break-downs. Okay? Can we agree on that, at least? Please?"

His lips twisted. She caught her breath in the event he grew fangs. Nothing happened for long moments. Except their breathing. The sound of their hearts beating. In perfect sync. She needed to stop envisioning that particular affectation. It was too weird.

"You feel good?" he finally asked.

"You are so gorgeous," she answered.

One of his eyebrows lifted, and he glanced away. His cheeks darkened as if he flushed.

Her canine teeth tingled oddly.

Leah ran her tongue along her upper teeth, and then chided herself for the instant need to check. Nothing was out of order. Everything felt exactly normal...in her mouth, anyway.

Anso turned back to her, affecting her without doing a thing. Leah's heart gave another couple of quick beats. *Damn thing.*

"My appearance...pleases you?"

"Well. Yeah. And then some."

"Some?"

"Yeah. As in...some more."

"More?"

Leah sighed. "And here I didn't think you suffered a Narcissistic Disorder."

He narrowed his eyes. His long dark lashes shadowed the light in them. That sent a rocket-load of sensation shooting through her innards. Leah's eyes widened.

"I do not understand," he told her.

"You've never heard of Narcissus? And Echo? The Greek legend?"

He shook his head.

"Really? Fine. I'll explain. Narcissus was a major babe in Ancient Greek mythology. He was totally hung up on himself. Wasted away staring at his image. Beautiful men are usually well aware of the fact they are beautiful. I've been with some, not nearly as handsome as you, but the signs are easy to recognize. They constantly check themselves out. You know...like in mirrors. Store windows. Anyplace with a reflection."

His expression cleared. And then he grinned. The rocket within her started spewing sparks. She tightened inner muscles against it.

"I do not have a reflection, *lioban.* But is it true? You find me thus?"

"Oh, brother. Since you're fictitious, I can say what I like, right? But don't push it. I'm not a fan of ego-stroking...but here goes. You have the kind of looks that stop traffic. Your body would shame a Grecian statue. And you're amazing in the sack, too."

"The sack?"

"What kind of lingo do they speak here? You don't know what that means, either?"

He shook his head.

"It means bed. And...any other place you can make love."

His grin widened. No fangs in sight.

*Good.*

"Ah. You speak of the act *semantwist.* And the wonder. I agree. You are also...amazing in the sack."

He ran his forefinger down her arm, lifting shivers. Leah looked at his finger and then back to his gaze. She'd been right. He had extremely dark, sable brown eyes, the color of his hair. Her heart gave another lurch. This was ridiculous.

"Nice," she finally replied.

"I must tell you, Leah. It is because you are my *weibchan.*"

"Oh. Yeah. Of course it is."

His finger stopped moving. "You know what that means?"

"Nope."

"I need to tell you...but I am a bit...hesitant."

"You? Hesitant?"

He nodded.

"Okay. I can look it up later."

"Look it up?"

"Oh. Come on. For the love of—! You don't know what that means either?"

"I am a ninth-century Germanic warlord, *lioban.* Your tone is an insult. If you were not my *weibchan* and beloved above measure, there would be consequences."

He'd gone still. Taut. Every muscle she could feel was rigid. The man looked feral and something else. He looked pretty damned scary. The sparks that had been shooting through her subsided, banked by his change in expression. Leah's eyes went so wide the air hurt. She blinked some moisture onto them before managing a swallow. Grasped at a straw.

"Come on, Anso. This is just too weird for me. You're saying you're what? Twelve hundred years old?"

"I will use your phrase. Yes, and then some," he replied.

"You are seriously expecting me to believe you're from the time of – oh! I don't know? Charlemagne?"

"Yes."

"Oh, Anso. Please. This is just too much. I mean, I was willing to accept that I'm suffering a hallucination on a grand scale. I was even willing to go Psychotic Delusion! But, no. Just no. You don't look a day past thirty-five."

"That is because I am a vampire."

"Damn it! That was a ground rule! Don't you obey the slightest thing?"

He lifted his upper lip in something that resembled a snarl, perfectly fitting the impression of bestiality. His look sent heat. All kinds of primitive emotions. She didn't find it remotely frightening, either. Everything on her body went alert. But damn everything! He had fangs again.

"All right! That's it. No fangs. That's a clear violation."

"Le...ah."

He broke her name in two like before with a lot of volume. The sound rattled more of the candles and something wooden creaked ominously. Leah pushed his arm and leg aside and sat up. *Weird.* Her abdomen muscles responded instantly and with a lot more strength than normal.

"Whatever that is supposed to do, it's broken. Okay? You've got a great voice. You know how to project it. All signs of Histrionic Disorder, by-the-way, but I am a little too hyped-up at the moment. Despite an ability that should have you on a stage somewhere, I am not amused. And you can just come out of the threatening stance, too. I don't allow that kind of thing in my life."

"I would never hurt you, *lioban.*"

He was beside her instantly, breathing with harsh gusts of air that matched hers. His eyes were tender. Warm. And looked nothing like an angry man. Her heart hurt. Her head wasn't far behind. *Great. Just great, Leah.* This delusion was taking a major downturn. That wasn't fair. This was her fantasy. She shouldn't have to deal with falling in love with a fictitious man – one who not only could demonstrate physical vampiric traits, which wasn't even possible for Schizophrenia – but might have just exhibited classic signs of Manic Depressive Disorder, too?

*Oh shit.*

What was wrong with her? She did not just think of love! Oh no. No. *No, Leah.* She didn't feel anything like that for Anso. *Just. No.*

A loud ringing sound split the silence that followed his statement. It was followed by the sound of wood splitting. Leah watched as one of his tables fell. The bed bounced, tilting the view, as Anso bolted from it.

"Where are you going?"

"That is the Sat phone. I must answer it."

"You have a satellite phone?" Her eyebrows rose.

"Yes."

He disappeared through a dark span of gloom that was an obvious doorway before she had a chance to ask why he didn't know what an online search meant if he had a Sat phone. Her mind was having trouble linking the words, anyway. He wasn't wearing anything and that view was something she'd never seen before. And pretty damn nice. Somewhere in college, she'd learned that the Ancient Greeks had run their Olympic races in the nude.

*Hmm.*

It was easy to see why.

Anso reappeared before she'd finished the thought, a large phone in his hand. She watched him punch some buttons. Blinked a couple of times in semi-disbelief. Not only at his speed – which she should be used to by now – but the man hadn't donned a scrap of fabric. The view from this side was even nicer than watching him running. He stuck the phone to his ear.

"Yes?"

*'Hello! Is this Anso?'*

*Oh.* Looked like more weirdness was on her plate this morning – if it was even really morning. She could hear the caller's voice. Easily. Clearly. It was a young male and he was rushing through his words. Or...he was from New York. She had several patients who hailed from New York. They all spoke in a rapid-fire fashion.

*'You took forever to answer, man. You are Anso? Yes? Come on, man! Speak up!'*

"Yes," Anso replied.

*'Great. Look. Nigel Beethan here. That won't mean anything to you. You've probably never even heard of me.'*

"No."

*'Okay. Well, I'm a Beethan, and one of the Hunter Beethan's, but I'm not a Beethan Hunter. Clear as mud?'*

"No. I mean yes."

*'Forget it! Listen. I'm Akron's assistant. I run the desk sometimes.'*

"Oh."

*'You really know how to fill airspace with words, don't you?'*

"What?" Anso asked.

*'Forget it. Not important. Look! I have a really big problem on my hands and a very small window of opportunity here. You're six foot five? Right?'*

"I am...not certain," Anso replied.

*'But you're a big guy, right? Your file sketch puts you at six foot five – maybe six foot six, and you look close to two hundred and...ninety, maybe?'*

"Pounds?"

*'Well...yeah. Duh.'*

Anso didn't like the fellow's tone. She watched him straighten. Flex a few muscles. Tighten more of them. It lifted a few things. The view was really incredible. Leah sighed. He sent a glance her way. Flushed again. Went back to his call. She was hard-put not to giggle.

"I am nineteen-and-a-half stone."

Six foot six – and whatever nineteen-and-a-half stone calculated to – looked really good to her. And here she'd thought Steve's firefighter brother was a god-among-mankind at six foot two and maybe two hundred.

*'Oh. Geez. Old farts! Ask a simple question; get a messed-up, archaic, non-calculable answer. The record says you were some kind of tribal warlord. Changed in 810. Right?'*

"Yes."

Leah gasped. It wasn't audible. And it was stupid. Anso's answer fit what he'd told her. It shouldn't be a surprise. She was in a delusionary hallucination. Things that happened should all add up. But the youthful male voice just kept spouting things she didn't have the imagination to conjure up.

*'It also says you were changed during a battle. Right? So...that means you're in the battle condition? Fit? Yes?'*

"Yes."

*'Sweet! Look, we've got an associate in trouble—!'*

"Get someone else," Anso interrupted in a commanding tone. One used to getting obeyed.

*'There is no one else!'*

"So?"

*'Come on, buddy. Didn't you hear me? I'm running the desk!'*

"So?" Anso repeated.

*'I need you to do something. How about if I make it an order?'*

"No."

Leah's eyebrows rose higher at the insubordinate word and Anso's tone.

*'Come on. Please? I'm begging here. You have to do it!'*

"I cannot."

*'Cannot? Or will not?'*

Anso looked across at her. His eyes glowed dark red again. An instant sense of warmth bloomed within her, as if the earlier sparks received an infusion of air. Leah had a difficult time gaining her next breath, and even then it was ragged. Raw.

"I have found my mate," Anso said.

Leah jerked. Her jaw dropped. Her heart pounded so loudly she almost missed the follow-up words. Her mind raced through possible explanations. Anso didn't mean that word the way it sounded. *No.* He couldn't.

He was using the word to mean physical joining. He did not mean lifetime companionship. That had to be the answer here.

The alternative was beyond frightening.

Because...*if* she'd somehow crossed into a fourth dimension, and Anso was a real vampire, would that mean the word mating meant *eternal* companionship?

'*Crap. Crap. Double crap. How far have you gone?*'

"She is not fully changed, if that is your question."

Anso might be speaking to the caller, but he was looking directly at her, leaving Leah no doubt whatsoever who he was addressing the answers to.

'*So she's half? So sorry, man. You'll have to leave her. That will be better, actually. It could be dangerous.*'

"You expect me to leave my mate?"

Anso was watching her as he said it. His look sent all kinds of signals her body had no trouble reading. All completely insane. Warmth enveloped her. Oh! If only she could shut her mind off and just go with the physical realm here! She wanted to...but, no. This was too much. She might have to do a complete paradigm shift. Evaluate things from a new perspective. Consider the unreasonable, despite how impossible it seemed.

This entire episode might be real.

It could actually be happening.

The warmth slowly dissipated, leaving her shaky. Cold. This was bad. At least if she'd gone insane, she knew what to do. There was a chance of recovery in her future. And the young male voice just kept adding more insanity to the mix.

'*You have to! You're old enough to have immunity to daylight and the weather satellite shows...crap. Crap. Crap. I'm not catching much of a break here. You're*' *getting high clouds. Slight chance of rain. She'll be safer where she is. Come on, man! Please? I'll do anything. Please?'*

Anso sighed heavily. "Who is my target?"

*'It's not a hit. We have a rogue. He's my responsibility...and damn me for being too blind not to see that trap before it sprang shut on me!'*

"Is it Hunters?"

*'I wish. Look. I'm sending details to your laptop. Airwaves are not secure enough for this. There! Done. Do this for me, man and I will so owe you. You have no idea...'*

The call ended because Anso pulled the phone away and flung it. The crash as it shattered was loud. Leah watched as he turned back to her. Folded his arms. Acted like he was fully dressed and this entire scenario was completely acceptable and normal.

"You heard?"

She nodded.

"You have questions for me?"

She licked her lips. Glanced away. Both signs of an upcoming lie. But maybe he didn't know that. She returned to meeting his look and tried to hold it. "None...that come to mind."

"I must go."

She nodded.

"You will stay here?"

Despite what Steven had said, she'd never been good at drama. Acting. Faking anything. She swallowed and glanced away again, this time into the upper left corner of the cavern. *Damn it!* It took an act of will to move her gaze back to his and nod.

"You give me your word?"

She had to settle for another nod. Any attempt at voicing words got stuck in her throat. He smiled. And then he moved.

# CHAPTER NINE

"How did you know I was lying?"

Anso sent a sidelong glance toward her. One of his eyebrows lifted, drawing her attention to his eyes. That was quite the affectation. He didn't need it.

"I was a leader of men. Bravery is often faked. Usually when facing a battle. When death is possible. There are signs."

"It's because I looked away, isn't it?"

"No." He shook his head as if it needed added emphasis.

"Then what?"

"Your heart sped up. Your breathing got shallow. You had to swallow often."

"How...do you know that?"

Her voice matched the sensation of incredulity. He gave her a swift grin before turning away. She followed his gaze. They looked over an old Soviet military complex. It was located on the Polish border, eighty-some-odd miles from Prague. She knew that because a helicopter had landed on an outcropping of rock outside Anso's hidden castle. They'd taken it. Some guy named Ivan piloted. Leah hadn't gotten a good look at him. She hadn't looked at much. The sun might be a no-show today, but it was almost blindingly bright. Excruciatingly hot. She'd hidden beneath a shawl and hung onto Anso while he explained. He couldn't just take a leap and they'd be at this camp. It was too far. He needed to reserve his strength.

That was another oddity in this dreamscape. Didn't vampires have unlimited strength? Wasn't that the mythos? And why did she even question it? Dreams, delusions and/or hallucinations had many nonsensical and unexplained things in them. That was one thing that came out in therapy sessions.

The view was desultory. What was once lush forest had been scarred with progress, but then it had been deserted. The forest was now winning. The place had been hard to spot. Here and there she could make out angular features that belonged to derelict, graffiti-strewn buildings. Strips of asphalt ribbed the ground in overgrown sections, while a multi-storied tower peeked from beneath a patchy covering of foliage. It was rusted. The entire area reeked of desolation. Decay. Rot.

"Because you are my *weibchan*. My every breath matches yours. As does each heartbeat. My pulse. It did then. It does now."

"Oh. No way."

"You deny the truth often, *lioban*."

"No. I deny science fiction that is presented as fact. Different concept entirely."

"Come. The guard is coming out again."

"Yeah. Looks like he's a chain-smoker."

"Where did you read that? It was not in the report."

Leah's heart stalled. Her mouth watered. "What...report?"

"The one I left open on my computer thing while I dressed and prepared."

"What makes you think I read it?"

He was pretty damned accurate about her physiological response to a lie attempt. He had the heart rate covered. The need to swallow. The pent-up breath. He regarded her for some moments while a smile played about his lips.

"What woman could resist?" he finally replied.

"Okay. So, maybe I peeked."

He grunted, grabbed her to his chest and sped through leaves that showered them with raindrops when jostled. His pace didn't have any steps to it. Good thing. Nigel's forecast hadn't been accurate. The skies were gray with clouds, each breath heavy with moisture, while the pelting of rain drowned out any other sound. She was grateful for Anso's assistance. Her skirt was made of burgundy-shaded velvet and nearly a foot too long. If this material got saturated, she'd have a hard time moving at all.

He stopped at a building edge. Knelt onto a knee and settled her atop his upraised thigh, inches away. Rain had plastered his dark hair to his skull. Rivulets drained down his pecs from where strips of hair clung to his shoulders. He was beyond gorgeous. He looked big, dark, sexy...

Dangerous.

Her heart gave a twinge. His eyes widened.

*Oh shit.*

He hadn't experienced that, too, had he? His words answered that. And her heart gave another lurch.

"I like your train of thought, *lioban.* If we had time. And a suitable spot. I would very much like to show you."

"Um. Anso?"

"Yes."

"It's not what you think."

He leaned forward to peer around the building edge. Straightened. Looked back at her.

"Is he still there?" Leah asked.

He nodded.

"I'm going to hamper this rescue, aren't I?"

"No."

"You should put me down. I'll be fine."

"Your skirt is too long. You'll trip."

"Who says I'll be moving anywhere?"

One of his eyebrows lifted.

"I wouldn't. I'd stay right here. Honest."

"No."

"Come on, Anso. I don't even know where I am! And look at me. I'm dressed like a—. A—. Oh! I don't know. A medieval princess or something."

"You look beautiful."

"Oh. Of course I do. To you. You're the guy who stocked all the wardrobe closets with really low-cut dresses that belong in a Renaissance Fair! And this shawl is useless! Look. It's pretty much see-through when wet."

"You did not wish to bring your jacket."

"That's because it's not mine. It belongs to Steven. My colleague. Or – he was my colleague. Remind me to send it to him if I don't wake up from this, okay?"

He grunted again.

"You know, I have a doctorate in psychology. You'd think I'd have the wits to envision efficient attire if I'm going to hallucinate! Especially if I'm going to be running through a forest in pouring rain, and traipsing through some heretofore unknown and secret deserted

Soviet military complex! That would be the smart move. I need cargo pants! Hiking boots. Thermal Henley. A water-resistant, fleece-lined jacket. With a hood. Yeah. *That* would work. And I have all that in my closet. I even bought short men's sizes, so I wouldn't have to go through a fat lady catalog to get them big enough. The outfit is brand new. Never worn – except for the jacket. One of my exes was the outdoorsy type. So I pretended."

He regarded her for long moments. "Why do you speak of all this?"

"I'm hoping it will trigger a wardrobe change."

He shook his head. "How so? And why? You look very beautiful."

"The translation of that is I look ridiculous."

"No. Perfect. But, I do apologize. You are a bit smaller than I anticipated. Everything will be too lengthy for you."

"Excuse me? Am I hearing right? You *anticipated?*"

"We are told about mates. I envisioned mine. I ordered all manner of attire, but you never arrived. So I gave up. Centuries ago." He looked around the corner again, his hand slowly reaching behind his back. "Have you ever handled a weapon?"

Her mouth had opened to start the denial, but he'd pulled a sharp dagger from the back of his trousers, silencing her. It had a black leather grip. A really long blade. Jagged-looking edges along one side. Looked extremely lethal. He held it out to her. Leah lifted both hands in the universal sign of defeat.

"This is too much for me, Anso. I mean, really. I'm a doctor of psychology. I don't do death and dismemberment. The most I've handled is a cooking knife. The occasional steak knife."

He secured the knife back behind him. "Very well. I will handle it. You stay at my side."

"Can't I just stay here?"

He gave her an unfathomable look. She tried desperately to keep her heart from beating any faster. Modulated her breath. Didn't even attempt a swallow. She didn't even move her gaze.

"I am sorry. I cannot leave you. It is too dangerous. Come. I will carry you."

He stood. Lifted her against his left side. Looked down at her, locking gazes. Her heart gave every sign of being affected as it thudded heavily. Rhythmically.

He was right.

There was a distinct echo as his heart matched.

"This isn't going to work," she whispered.

"Wrap your arms about my neck. Legs about my waist. Hold tight."

"How are you going to get him to go with you? Nigel says he's your size. Angry. Stubborn. You can't force him if you're holding me."

She did the requested movements while she argued. Got suctioned into place against his side. And it felt really nice. Damp, but warm.

"That is the least of our trouble. You saw the plan?"

"Vaguely. Something with 'D's."

"Yes. Four of them."

"That's not a bra size?"

"Why would it be such a thing?"

"Delusions have a way of being off-the-wall like that."

"This is not a delusion, *lioban*. A 4-D Team is scheduled for noon. We have less than an hour."

"Before what?"

He looked down at her. Lifted both eyebrows, putting little lines across his forehead. Replied with one word. "Boom."

"Boom?"

"Deploy. Destroy. Disinfect. Disappear."

"Destroy? How much destruction are we talking?"

"Everything."

"You're joking."

He shook his head.

"You can't just blow everything up! Not in my delusion! That kind of thing will really do some damage to my psyche!"

"I speak, but you do not seem to hear. This is not a delusion, *lioban.*"

"It has to be."

"Why?"

"Because anything else is impossible."

"How so?"

"We really have to go into this now? Right now?"

"We have a few moments. The guard is still there. And even if he moves, I can go through a door as easily as open it."

"All right. Fine. I'll just start with that. You'll go *through* a door?"

"Yes."

"Let me guess. Because you're a vampire."

He smiled.

"Let's start there, shall we? We can drill down from that. There's a root cause to this hallucination. I might as well find it before we blow stuff up. You claim to be a vampire. You actually exhibit vampiric traits. Both are impossible."

"Why do you say that?"

"Because it's true."

"What makes it true?"

Leah blinked. Thought for a moment. "Because it just is."

"Again. Why?"

"Certain beings do not exist. Never have. Werewolves. Yetis. Vampires. Easter bunnies. Tooth fairies. You know. Impossible things."

"Why do you say they don't exist?"

"Because nobody ever saw one!"

"They have."

"Bull crap. If they had, there would be a valid record."

"Every culture has written proof of their existence."

"Mythical stories. Complete fiction."

"What makes them fictional?"

"There is no scientific proof to back anything up."

"What would you need for this scientific proof?"

"Okay. Maybe if I met one. Saw signs of special powers. Proof of immortality. Got bitten by one. Or maybe—"

Her voice stopped. He had one eyebrow quirked up again.

"If I cut myself right now and it instantly heals, would that suffice as scientific proof?"

She was going to gag. "No. Please. Don't do that."

"You worry for no reason. But you are amusing." He leaned forward and looked around the building again. Returned. "You are ready?"

"Just don't kill anybody. Okay? Don't make me go there! Killing people in your mind is the sign of a truly deranged psyche!"

"*Lioban.* This is not in your mind."

"Please, Anso?"

"You make this extremely difficult for us. Do you know what you ask?"

"Please? If I cross that line, there's no going back! Please?"

He considered her for a moment, as if she asked something completely unreasonable. And then he sighed heavily.

"Very well. No killing. For you."

The relief was short-lived. Anso was moving before the words finished making sound. They should have gone around. Used the hulking chunks of concrete buildings for cover. They traversed an old courtyard. Thick layers of gravel appeared to have impeded plant growth. There wasn't any cover except the rain. Leah couldn't seem to move her gaze, or even close her eyes, despite sending the order for both. The guard looked up. Saw them. Chucked his cigarette to reach for the gun over his shoulder.

Leah sucked in a breath. Watched as Anso back-handed him across the chest. The guard smacked into the wall and slumped to the ground, on his front, looking broken. Anso shoved him with a boot toe. The man groaned and then went silent.

"He's still...alive?" she whispered.

"Yes."

"Okay. Thank you." She hiccupped as she exhaled.

Anso didn't wait to hear it. They were already inside the door, facing what looked like miles of metal-sheathed tunnel. The ground was earthen. Dark. Damp. It was instantly much quieter. Anso gripped her tighter to his left side and leapt forward. And then he was flying.

Literally.

The air was immediately cold. Brisk. It whipped at her clothing and hair, drying both. The ribbed tunnel blurred into a solid stream of dull silver tones. She watched it happen.

That still didn't mean she had to believe it.

# CHAPTER TEN

Anso had never fought under restrictions like this. Always before, he'd killed without compunction. Used his bow for distance shots. Hacked his way with sword and dagger at close range. He'd taken on multitudes with pleasure. Left a bloodbath. It was his signature. The larger the horde facing him, the better he liked it. Centuries had passed while his hits raised barely an eyebrow. Now – depending on the country - an assignment could engender all manner of unwanted scrutiny. Global news coverage. His assassinations could usually be attributed to war. Men always seemed to fight for the same reasons. Resources such as farming land. Water. Precious minerals. Religion. And power. Somebody was always trying to subdue someone else. Humankind just couldn't seem to get along with each other...but that did offer a lot of perfect killing ground.

His head grazed the line of fluorescent tube lighting as he flew. The complication of leaving his foes breathing added an edge of danger he hadn't felt in millennia. His pulse ramped up. His muscle went taut. His breathing quickened, each one was deeper and heavier, air filling his lungs before he expelled it. This sensation was heady.

Exciting.

Addictive.

A large fence blocked further passage, backed by two guards. A dog. They had a camp stove burning. One man waved his hands above it, warming them. Anso's approach wasn't even noticed. He yanked Leah more tightly against him, turned, and slammed through the obstruction with his right shoulder. One guard got enmeshed in chain-link, rendering him useless, semi-conscious, but alive. The other ricocheted off a wall. The camp stove went flying, spewing heated coals that sputtered and sizzled. Neither man got a shot off. The dog didn't react.

Anso could hear the next batch of guards. Talking. Laughing. They didn't have any reaction to having security breached. Because they were at least a hundred yards away. Whatever organization manned this complex, the leaders needed a course on military strategy. The guard stations were spaced too far apart. They were obviously not expecting trouble, and if it came, they were counting on an alarm being given.

And they were lax.

Anso stopped at a corner, pulled in a breath. Held it. And then peeked. He had three men to get through next. They stood in a semi-circle around another stove, warming hands. Humans and their frailties. Anso wasn't remotely cold. Then again, the excitement of this venture might be cancelling sensations such as temperature.

One guard scratched at his groin before hefting his gun into a more comfortable position on his shoulder. The other two were unarmed, their weapons leaning up against the wall behind them. No dogs. Leah was breathing rapidly, but nothing that troubled. She was the perfect companion.

Anso leaned over to her ear.

"I must do this on my own, *lioban.*"

Anso whispered it before loosening his arm. He settled her on the ground beside him. Smiled at what looked like real concern in her eyes.

"I will come back for you. Please. Stay here."

She tilted her head. Anso took it for agreement. And moved.

He leapt into the midst of the guards. Kicked the armed man into the fellow standing beside him. The hit probably broke bone, as did the landing, but he wasn't slicing off heads. Nothing appeared lethal. The next guard got back-handed into the opposite wall. This mode of warfare was beginning to be enjoyable as well as exciting. Anso was grinning as Leah reached him, holding a wad of skirts in her arms.

His grin faded as she looked up at him.

"You are...well?" he asked with a whisper.

She looked over the three guards as if assessing mortality rate. And then she looked back up at him. The mass of fabric in her arms looked unwieldy. It also drew attention to her bosom. Anso swallowed and looked away before the lust for battle turned into something else.

She was just so womanly!

So fair!

So endearing.

With a sigh, Anso pulled her close and hugged her to him. The move lifted her. He bent to press a kiss to the top of her head. She was the perfect heft. Size. Weight.

"You handle yourself well, *weibchan.*"

"What?"

"You have done this before?"

"Done what?"

"Gone into battle."

"Battle? Right. This? Well...it's a lot like watching a movie, but it's not that bad. I mean no one is bleeding yet."

Anso smiled. "True."

"Look. I had a boyfriend who was a fighter. The hard-core kind. Bare fisted. No holds barred. He won the Thursday Night Fights once."

His eyebrows rose. "You seem to wish my anger, *lioban*. That is unreasonable, as well as impossible. I find you too wondrously fair. The greatest gift. And I am your willing admirer."

"I wish your anger? Why on earth would you say that?"

"You mention prior men in your life to me. You do it...oft."

"Oh. I do not."

He lifted an eyebrow. She blinked a few times.

"Look. Anso. If I did something like that, it might be a sign of self-esteem issues. Relational problems. Sufferers don't feel attractive, so they continually bring up prior relationships as proof of their desirability. It makes for some bad dating experiences. I deal with this kind of thing a lot in my practice."

"This is an issue with you?"

"Heck no."

"You are certain?"

Her face went completely expressionless. "Why don't we just get back to you handling the knock-down/drag-out portion of this rescue, and leave the psychoanalysis to me. Okay?"

He considered her for a long moment. Listened to her heart beating in rhythm with his. Thought about asking the definition of that word before deciding it was of little importance. His mate was perfection. Womanly beauty personified. It didn't matter if she worried over it or not. He had eternity to make certain she knew the truth.

He finally nodded.

"All right, then. Let's get cracking. We don't have time for this right now, anyway."

"Cracking?"

"It means get going. Fire up the jets. You know – move."

"Why do you not just say that?"

"Good question. I don't have an answer right now. Maybe because it grounds me. Makes me feel normal in an abnormal situation. I don't know. I'll figure it out later. If I'm still stuck in this delusion, that is."

"This is not a delu—"

"Don't say it, okay? Just. Don't."

Anso shook his head at her stubbornness, before picking her back up and moving. The next challenge was another trio of guards, this one situated even farther down the tunnel. A quick scan of their area showed them just as unprepared and lax. Two played cards. One doodled in the earthen floor with a knife blade. Nobody wore a gun at their shoulder.

Anso swiveled and set Leah down. Met her gaze. Lifted his brows. She nodded. He didn't wait another moment. He launched into the midst of guards, scattering the cards. A kick sent one guard toward a wall. He back-handed the other into unconsciousness before making a fist. That hit broke the fellow's jawbone, barely managing to keep from killing him.

But Anso hadn't been quick enough. The fellow had struck with his knife. The blade had found an open spot on his side. Just above the belt. Anso grunted. Leah raced to him. Looked at the knife. Back to his face. And then she started hyperventilating, dragging his every breath into sync.

And he had to change that.

"Calm, little one."

"But, Anso! You've been stabbed!"

"Leah. Please."

The rate of her breathing made him dizzy. Weakened his limbs. Added difficulty without reason. Anso groaned as he reached over, grabbed the hilt now slippery with blood, and yanked the knife out. He tossed it. Red fluid spewed outward before he could get a palm in place to clamp. Squeeze. The sight of so much blood affected him, however. He wasn't strong enough at the moment to fight against it. His canines tingled and then elongated. Thirst grew in his mouth. It almost overrode the pain of his injury. Fiery sensation shot through him even as he realized it should probably hurt more. And Leah wouldn't cease hyperventilating. Anso swayed slightly. Locked his knees to remain upright. Tightened the arm about her. Shook her slightly.

"Leah. Stop this! Please? You must...calm yourself. Breathe...normally."

"Oh, Anso! You're wounded! That's a lot of blood! You're going to die!"

He smiled down at her, but it was probably a grimace. His fangs were on full display, too.

"I am...immortal, *lioban*. Please. I beg you. Calm yourself. This is nothing."

Her eyes went huge. She sucked in a breath. And then – thank the gods – she held it for a few moments before easing air back out. Her next breath was slower. The next followed it. And the next. His legs quit trembling. His vision cleared.

"You really...aren't going to die?" she whispered.

"No."

"Promise?"

He twisted. Lifted his hand. The wound had already ceased bleeding. It was starting to knit. She viewed it then looked up at him with an expression of astonishment.

"It's healing!"

Her whisper was loud. He almost shushed her, but it wasn't necessary. The guards were stationed too far apart to hear. And her astonishment was like music to his ears. She had no choice but to believe him now.

"Yes," he finally answered.

"Oh, no. No. No. Just...no."

"Hang on, my love. It is almost over."

She stiffened. He looked back at her. She wouldn't meet his eyes. She appeared to focus on his neck armor. "What is it?"

"You just called me...your love."

"Yes. I did. Because you are."

"Anso."

She started trembling. He moved closer. She stepped a corresponding distance back. Anso had to look aside for a moment. Blink against a stab of something at his eyes that he'd never admit. She was holding her mass of skirts to her breast, almost like a shield.

"I do not understand, Leah. I have called you that since we met. That is what *lioban* means. I told you as much. Remember?"

"I know. It just sounds...so different in English. Like it's *real*."

Anso rolled his eyes and slowly shook his head. "Women. I shall never understand them. I swear. You ready to go, then? We are almost there."

"How do you know that?"

"There was a chart in the file. You didn't note it?"

"I was spying! Okay? People who are being sneaky are usually being hasty, too. They're afraid of getting caught! I didn't see everything. Okay?"

Anso started to chuckle, but caught it in the event she took offense. His mate was thoroughly amusing. Entertaining. And completely engaging. He couldn't wait to finish this, and show her just how much.

# CHAPTER ELEVEN

The man they were supposed to rescue didn't look like he expected one. Or desired it, for that matter.

*Actually...*

Leah narrowed her eyes against the onslaught of light. After the fairly dim span of tunnels they'd sped through, the room they found themselves in was overly bright. Painted a perky shade of yellow that was almost cheerful. She trailed Anso as he chucked the last guard into the room ahead of them. The man grunted as he hit a bench, and then subsided to the floor, proving not only that he probably still lived, but Anso wasn't experiencing any weakness from his wound, either.

Leah glanced at Anso's side. Her heart gave a huge throb. Her knees wobbled. She stumbled, the move dropping her skirts.

*Oh. My. Stars.*

Anso didn't have a wound! There was just a lot of blood where he'd been stabbed. And it wasn't dry. Her upper teeth tingled as if that meant something. Leah ran her tongue along them just to make sure everything was normal and sane, and then she looked at the man they'd come to rescue. Her tongue stalled. Her jaw slackened. And everything else came to a jerking halt.

There was a fellow at the far end of the room, almost a perfect match to Anso in size and age. He looked them over for a span before his upper lip lifted in a sneer. It was an insolent gesture. Coming from a god-like position. He was sitting in a chair – a really large chair. It had been set atop concrete blocks, making it appear even larger. Throne-like. As if a king sat there.

The report she'd glimpsed hadn't been enough preparation for this! She'd scanned the screen of Anso's laptop. She'd seen the words Viking. Icelandic. Large. She didn't know they'd meant the equivalent of the Norse god, Thor.

And the report said he had an identical twin?

*Holy shit.*

Seeing two of these guys at the same time would be grounds for swooning.

If she hadn't met Anso, this guy would have been unbelievable...except, maybe at an Olympic-level wrestling event. He wore a sleeveless leather tunic trimmed with ermine. Large embossed silver bands encased his biceps, showing off muscle definition. His knee-high leather boots were trimmed with the same fur as his tunic. That attire put a lot of thigh on display. It was as muscled as the rest of him. A large sword rested negligently in his hand, tip down, almost boring into a concrete block. His hand tightened on the hilt as he stood. The chair creaked. Leah's jaw finished dropping. And she wasn't even into blondes.

But she knew a major babe when she saw one.

This guy was major league babe. Why...if she hadn't had her fantasy man brought to life in the physical form of Anso, she'd be salivating here.

*Okay.*

It would probably be closer to drooling.

He stepped down off his pedestal, placing him on the same level as Anso. There he stopped, matching Anso in posture. The two men just stood, tensing muscles while they faced each other, sizing each other up. There was a distinct vibe running through the room. It carried emotion. Threat. Tons of testosterone. Shivers ran her skin as she sensed it. Leah looked from Thor to Anso and back to Thor, wondering if she was about to see a male pissing match come to life here.

"You are Athlerod?" Anso asked.

"Who are you?"

"Anso."

"Are you a Hunter?"

"Why? Were you expecting one?"

"You're from VAL, then?"

"Yes."

"I'm not going back."

"Nobody asked you to."

Athlerod grunted. He sounded a lot like Anso when he did it. It must be a male thing. A big-guy, male thing. Leah looked away before they saw her expression.

"What country spawned you?" Athlerod asked.

"None."

"You're not a vampire?"

"I didn't say that."

"What did you say?"

"It was not a country back then."

"Do you even know?"

Anso breath hitched slightly before resuming. Leah knew it because hers did the same thing. He didn't give any other sign that the comment bothered him.

"I was a chieftain. Germanic. We didn't have a name. We didn't need one."

Leah's brows lifted. Anso hadn't told her his title, but she'd suspected royalty. Too bad she wasn't a history aficionado. She'd know for certain what he spoke of.

"Were you a Teuton?"

"That is one of the names history has given us."

"Really? Well...we used to gather our slaves from your tribes. Sold them in the caravan cities. Made a lot of gold."

*Whoa.*

Athlerod's comment was designed to get a negative reaction. It matched his stance, and his air of defiance. Her first impression had been wrong. The blonde fellow lacked maturity. He wasn't near Anso's age. She'd guess mid-twenties – at most. And it was growing obvious to her. He was suffering. She just didn't know why, or what, or how deeply. Leah noted that Anso stiffened slightly at the insult. That was the only physical sign.

"I thought you were an Icelandic Viking," he finally replied.

"Yeah. So?"

"Icelanders were not the scourge of the forest zones. It was the Swedes. We called them *Rus*."

*Oh! Cool.* She hadn't known that, either. She supposed that was how Russia got its name.

"Are you calling me a liar?"

Athlerod took a step away from his chair. Anso folded his arms as if he faced a selection of wares for purchase, not an arrogant, aggressive Viking in the prime of life. One, furthermore, who was obviously spoiling for a fight. Leah just couldn't decide if he liked fighting and Anso was a distinct challenge, or if he suffered a Borderline Personality Disorder. That might explain why he was exhibiting such aggressive tendencies.

"No," Anso replied.

"Are you that weak, old man?" Athlerod countered.

"You have a strange attitude for a youngster."

"Young? Who are you calling young? I was turned in the year 985."

"810," Anso replied.

*Oh. Brother.* Looked like the pissing match was still on and happening.

"I can still take you."

"Is that what you want? Another fight?"

"Well, at least this time I might have a challenge, although you are a lot older than I'm used to."

*Another insult?*

Leah watched Anso absorb it, and then ignore it. A sense of pride swelled within her at watching him. That was ridiculous. The entire episode was. But, it fit perfectly with a delusion. Very little made sense until you listed things, sectioned them for analysis, and assigned reason. This particular delusion was going to take any psychologist's entire career to figure out.

"Wasn't your performance two nights past enough for you?" Anso finally asked with a nonchalant tone.

"You heard about that?"

"Why else would I be here?"

"You came because I won the Underground Fight?"

Anso chuckled. "I don't care how many fights you start, Athlerod. I don't even care how many you win. You're a vampire. Winning against a human is a foregone conclusion."

"I didn't do it for the win."

"Then, why did you do it?"

Athlerod lifted his sword toward Anso. Bent his knees slightly, and shuffled a step nearer. "I don't have to answer that. Now. Get your sword out, old man."

"We don't have time for this."

"You scared?"

"Not hardly."

"Then why won't you fight me?"

"I told you. We don't have time. Now come."

"You expect me to go with you without a fight?"

"Yes."

"Forget it. You can just go back to Akron and tell him I'm not interested."

"Akron didn't send me."

"Really? Then, who did?"

"Nigel."

Athlerod looked surprised for a moment and then he started chuckling. It took a few moments before he sobered enough to explain. "Well. I can see why he didn't come himself."

"Really? Why?"

Athlerod gave Anso a deadpan expression. "He's a pipsqueak. A large breath will knock him over."

"He is running the desk."

"Yeah. So? What is that supposed to mean? You think I'm afraid of him?"

"No, but you should be."

"Why?"

"You garnered attention."

"Not the right kind, obviously. And not enough."

*Whoa. Leah.*

That answer was a distinct clue. Athlerod wanted attention. He didn't care what kind he got, negative or positive. Both were signs of a Borderline Personality Disorder. There was a root cause. Since he was vampiric, she could probably rule out substance abuse or medical condition. That left traumatic event. Now, she just needed to find out what it was.

"You wish attention? Is that why you took on forty-one fighters, one-at-a-time?"

"I took on forty-*two* fighters! All at the same time! Why do you think I got arrested?"

"You are not under arrest."

Athlerod straightened. Frowned. "What do you call this?"

"A bidding war. With you as the prize."

"What?"

"You don't understand?"

Athlerod shook his head.

"Your performance got attention, all right. You have eight Fight Managers haggling over you. The World Wrestling Federation is on its way here with a contract offer, and at least two countries are sending representatives from their Olympic Committees."

"That's stupid. The Czech Republic already has me."

"They got out-bid early. Now, they're just holding out for the highest bidder."

"Really? That's...fantastic news! Better than I hoped! I'll be famous! Beethan's Hunters can't possibly fail to hear about me!"

"Organized sports have medical tests."

"So?"

"You are a vampire. Your blood cannot be tested!"

"Better and better!"

"Stupid fool! You are part of a covert organization. There are consequences to what you have done."

"Are you here to carry them out?"

"If necessary."

"Good. That works, too."

The man lifted his sword and this time he slashed the air with it. Leah was looking at a severe case of Intermittent Explosive Disorder, brought on to cause harm – mostly to himself. But...the root question was why?

*Why?*

Anso failed to take the bait again. He looked at the Viking for long moments and then sighed. "We really don't have time for this."

"Make time!"

Athlerod lunged forward and swung his sword. Leah's cry was cut off by the ringing sound of blade upon blade. Anso had freed his weapon with a lightning-quick move and he used it to defend. Countless times. Against multiple blows. And then he attacked. Leah hadn't stayed around to watch the first of it. She'd grabbed up her skirts, raced to the concrete blocks, climbed them, and then stood in the chair. She was out of danger, but situated perfectly for observing. The men looked equal on so many fronts: Fitness level. Training. Expertise with a sword. They continually hammered at each other, their movements encompassing the entire span of floor space. Muscles strained. Grunts filled the room. They were interspersed with the continual ringing sound of steel against steel. That was loud. It echoed.

And this was getting serious.

Anso was going to win. She watched the battle tip his way. He had experience. It showed. His blows began to back up the Viking. And then he used his hilt for hitting. Athlerod took a blow to his arm that stunned. His sword arm lowered. That gave Anso an opening for a blow to the Viking's chin.

The man went down heavily. Onto his back. Although only a hint of a thudding sound accompanied it. Anso was atop him, a knee on the Viking's chest and his blade pressed against the other man's throat.

"Wait! Anso! No! Wait!"

*Stupid dress.*

Leah grabbed the wad of velvet and jumped down. Her feet stung. Her thighs jiggled. Her breasts nearly fell from the bodice. She ignored all of that to reach Anso. She grabbed his sword arm with both hands and hung on.

"Please. Wait!"

Anso turned his head to regard her. He didn't release the Viking. And Athlerod wasn't any help. He looked up at her with vivid ice-blue eyes. Then he winked. And spoke. His throat immediately welled blood from a thin slice across it from Anso's blade.

"Who is the *vif*?" Athlerod asked.

*Vif* must be another word for female. Leah wasn't asking. She didn't care.

"My mate," Anso replied.

"Truly? Lucky *pokker*. She is very beautiful. Lush. Soft. Womanly." And then he growled as if for emphasis.

His motions brought more blood to the cut on his throat. He swallowed, and it started pooling. And then it began to drip off both sides. Leah couldn't seem to move. Her breath quickened. Her mouth watered. Her teeth started tingling again. Leah forced her gaze away. Back to Athlerod's. She regarded him for long moments as he did her. She squeezed her hands on Anso's bicep. He eased up his pressure.

She had another big, brawny, beautiful man claiming she was the epitome of womanhood? She'd obviously been born in the wrong century.

*And here I thought I was fat.*

"I know," Anso replied finally.

Athlerod didn't move his gaze. He was still entirely focused on her. And his eyes looked a bit moist. He blinked often. And then sighed.

"My brother found his mate, too. But she is a *stick*."

The description was said in a desultory fashion, denigrating fashion models everywhere. Leah's lips twitched at the instant thought. And then Anso replied, and stole her breath. Her wits. Her voice.

"I think you will find when your mate appears...that no matter what her shape, or height, or coloring...she will be the most beautiful creature in existence."

Leah's eyes filled. Athlerod's features blurred as she blinked back the emotion. Anso so rarely linked many words together, and the ones he'd just spoken filled her with light. Joy. She probably glowed.

"Yeah? Well, she is also treacherous. Worse than a *Midgard* serpent."

"Did this happen...recently?" Leah asked in a soft tone.

"*Ja.*"

"Your twin...was always with you, wasn't he?"

"Again *ja.* So?"

"Oh, Athlerod. I can help you."

"I don't need help."

"You were with your twin for over a thousand years, weren't you?"

"Your mate is very nosy."

Athlerod turned to address Anso. Leah moved her hands to his head and pulled him back to face her.

"You know. I am about done with male machismo bullshit. This is my psychotic delusion, and I'm running the show."

His eyebrows rose. Anso choked.

"You are suffering Separation Anxiety Disorder, young man. It is manifesting in anger. And self-hatred. You are actually trying to commit suicide, but you are too weak to do it yourself."

He stiffened. Anso's knee flexed to hold him down.

"I am a professional! Get it? I can help. If you make an appointment—"

She didn't get the rest out. A series of tremors raced through the ground, jostling everything in the room. Leah flew upward. Anso grabbed her waist and yanked her to him. Hugged her tight. Everything stationary became a projectile. Athlerod's body heaved upward before being jettisoned into the cement blocks that had comprised his pedestal. And then the walls started wavering. Large cracks opened up.

"What in *hel*?"

Athlerod sounded more angry than hurt.

"I love you, Leah," Anso told her.

"What?"

"I told you. We did not have time."

"What are you telling me now?"

His gaze locked to hers. Her heart dropped.

"Boom," he replied.

More tremors shook the room. Chunks of debris rained down on them. Anso tucked her into his chest and leaned forward, his body taking blow after blow with an occasional grunt.

"We're going to die?"

Athlerod yelled the question. His voice was disjointed, as if he yelled from another room.

"Isn't this what you wanted?" Anso shouted back.

"No!"

Something large hit Anso, dropping them to the floor. He wrapped his body about Leah, absorbing even more blows. The space darkened by the moment. Grew heavy with dust. It was difficult to breathe.

And then a voice spoke through the destruction happening all about them. A large voice. Deep. Resonant with all manner of bass tones. Beyond anything she'd ever heard.

"Anso! Athlerod! Get in the earth. Drill down. Leah? Come with me."

"No!"

Her denial didn't make sound. Arms reached for her, yanked her away from Anso and into complete blackness. It enveloped her. Impenetrable. Inexorable.

And absolutely inescapable.

# CHAPTER TWELVE

A phone rang.

The sound grated. Loud. Harsh.

When the noise stopped, that wasn't the end of it, however. All manner of clicks and pings and humming noises invaded her consciousness, probably emitting from electrical devices. At various decibel levels. Some male spoke out in the halls somewhere. Got answered with a burst of feminine laughter. That was odd. She'd chosen this condominium unit after a lot of research. The architect had taken acoustical site design into account, including placement of windows, balconies, courtyards. The construction included soundproofing concepts in the ceilings, floors, and walls. She shouldn't be able to hear anything outside of her unit that easily.

The telephone rang again interrupting her train of thought. It also made her jump slightly. Her ears were ringing by the time it finished. And then she heard something really strange. She could swear she heard the long clicking sound that accompanied a resident accessing the security door at night.

From down a long hall? And three stories below her?

Leah lifted her head. Blinked and looked out her bedroom door into her living area.

*It was true. She was home.*

But something was really odd here. She still possessed incredible vision to match her hearing. She could see every facet of her home. Her condo was an open concept, the space outside comprising living and dining rooms, along with the kitchen. She'd liked that. Now, it was inundating her with information. She noted lines of grout between the floor tiles, the porous nature of the paint on the walls. No wonder she always had to wash it! Even now, she noted a slight smudge just above one of the light switches. And then she noted the kitchen! *Ugh.* She liked her home immaculate. Orderly. Uncluttered. She'd cleaned it before she left for the conference. She'd been lax. There was a large smear of something on the front of the oven, and the refrigerator door handle needed a good washing.

Another phone ring sounded. Leah grimaced until it ended, only to be bombarded with the sound of her answering machine. It was set at jet engine sound level. She listened to her voice with hunched shoulders. *Wow.* Her greeting wasn't personable and approachable. She sounded clinical, non-emotional, and slightly metallic. Like an extension of the machine.

"You've reached the residence of Doctor Thurman. I'm not here right now, but if you leave your name and number, along with a brief message, I shall endeavor to return your call."

There was an annoyingly brisk beep. And then her colleague Steven started yelling. She almost covered her ears. She'd rarely heard him raise his voice.

"Leah? I just got your message with my coat from the drycleaners. You could have just told me you felt ill and took an early flight back to the states! You didn't have to leave me hanging for almost thirty hours, worried to death! I even contacted the US Embassy! And those jerk-offs said they couldn't do anything for at least another day! And then, they'd look into a possible disappearance. You have no idea—! Look. It's eight a.m. over here. We're six hours different. Sorry. It's the middle of the night. We'll discuss it on Wednesday when I get—."

The connection ended, stopping Steven's tirade. He hadn't needed to shout. Then again...maybe she should factor in her acute hearing issues right now. He might not have been that loud.

Leah's head dropped back to her pillow.

So.

It had happened.

She'd awakened from the delusion. And she was in a familiar place. Atop her bed. In her condo. Completely safe. If a bit chilled. Even her mental facilities appeared intact. She should feel relieved. Perhaps a bit anxious. Worried. Maybe weak. Anything but what she really felt.

Like crying.

Leah blinked against a sudden sting of tears. Held her breath while shivers ran down her arms. Eased the air back out. Somehow conquered the desire to weep. And felt like celebrating that small win. She'd come to her senses, but the path to wellness wasn't going to be an easy one. Recovery for patients who suffered delusions and hallucinogenic episodes was as varied and personal as the episode itself. Some patients didn't recall anything. Hypnosis was the usual method of bringing out their experience so it could be treated. Some patients recalled bits and pieces of their experience, and those would hit at random, sometimes inopportune moments. Other patients recalled everything. They could dictate what had happened to them item by item. In the event of a traumatic-event-initiated delusion, those were frightening. Because the details were always at the forefront of the sufferer's mind. In horrific detail. Accepting that, dealing with the fear and living with it, became the patient's new reality. Often, they needed pharmaceutical help.

She could see why now.

Leah sat up.

Looked like her experience was going to fit in the last category. She'd been away from reality for a span of thirty hours. It sure felt like a lot more time than that had elapsed.

Thirty hours.

*Of absolute paradise.*

She wasn't going to discuss this with Steven. Not on Wednesday. Not ever. It had been too vivid. Much too real. She remembered everything. Perfectly. With great wonder. Her heart rate picked up as she remembered those last moments. When Anso had held her and told her he loved her.

And she hadn't told him the same.

Leah wiped a sudden tear away.

*Not good.*

She was too emotional for this. She couldn't possibly love a man who didn't exist except in her mind. The potential for disaster was too high. Bereavement carried all kinds of emotional trauma. Leah wiped away another tear. And then another. This was bad. She'd never felt so alone! As if she'd lost a part of herself. A necessary one.

She forced her mind to handle simple tasks. Start small. She needed a tissue. They were in the bathroom. She rolled to her back, sat up, scooted to the side of her bed, and looked down at the maroon velvet dress she still wore.

Shock was an icy sensation.

Her veins filled with it as she looked up, directly into the mirror atop her bureau. Her face should have reflected shock. Astonishment. Distress. It didn't. Leah narrowed her eyes on her image and couldn't see a damned thing that mattered. Oh. She could see the wall behind her perfectly, the picture she'd hung of a sunset at sea. She'd bought it for its restful qualities. The light wood of her headboard was distinct and easily picked out. But she was a large gray blob. She tried twisting. Turning. Sticking her arms out. She stood. Did a couple of jumping jacks. Nothing worked. She was still just a large gray-shaded blob. All she'd proved was it moved.

This was not happening. Not to her. She'd heard of this. She'd never dealt with it. Sometimes patients suffered continual setbacks. Their delusionary state came and went, seemingly with impunity. Those were the people usually destined for the insane asylums.

*No.*

*Not her.*

Leah tripped, before remembering the stupid skirts were too long. All of them. She wore two. One burgundy velvet. The one beneath it was silk and stuck to the velvet with static electricity. She probably sent sparks every time she moved. It hadn't bothered her before. And it didn't now. The innermost layer was a long linen underskirt thing. Leah grabbed the armful of the skirts and marched into her living area. First things first. She was chopping a foot of material off. And she had sewing scissors in a basket at the end of her sofa.

*Crap.*

She'd lent the basket to Steve's wife.

*Fine.*

She had knives in her kitchen. Just like she'd told Anso.

Her heart thudded painfully at the recollection. Her breath caught. A shivery sensation shot down her legs. Leah grabbed the edge of her counter and scowled at it, and somehow managed to stanch any further reaction to the thought of him as she recovered from these.

This was bad.

Really bad.

Just thinking of him brought about this severe a physical response? She really needed to get a grip here. He wasn't real. She wasn't in love. And even if she was in love, the feelings shouldn't hit this hard. Anso didn't exist. The effect of being without him didn't exist, either. It wasn't real.

*There.*

Reasonable. Sane. Logical.

She pulled the knife drawer out with too much strength. Kitchen blades of all kinds scattered across the floor. She hadn't realized she owned so many. Leah knelt, selected a large one with a serrated edge, dropped the skirts, and started hacking.

And slipped.

The knife sliced across her thumb pad, nearly into her wrist. Leah looked at the cut with horror even as blood welled. She instinctively stuck it to her lips. Tasted. And then sucked with abandon. Her legs wavered for an entirely different reason. She'd never tasted anything so exquisite. An explosion of delight erupted in her mouth.

She fell.

The skirts absorbed most of the impact, but she'd lost contact with her wrist. Leah was moving it back to her mouth when she noticed something truly astonishing.

The wound was closing! Before her eyes!

*Oh, shit.*

*Oh, shit.*

*Oh, shit.*

The sensation of shock was just as icy as before. She was more than taken-aback. She was surprised. Stunned. And amazed. If she had a reflection, the one in the glass-front of her oven would have shown what a flabbergasted expression looked like. But she was just a big blob.

*Wait.*

What had Anso and Nigel spoken of? During that weird sat phone call? Hadn't there been something said about how she'd been half-turned but not fully? Was that even possible?

*No, Leah. Just no.*

She grabbed the skirts and stood up. Without once using something to hold to. Her legs had never been this sturdy. Or strong. Was she hallucinating here? Or was this real? Leah considered her countertop for a moment. It was constructed from granite, or a good facsimile of it. This called for an equivalent of the pinch test. She pulled in a breath and smacked a palm down onto the counter. A plethora of fractures in the granite radiated outward from her hand, accompanied by cracking sounds. And it hadn't even hurt.

*Holy shit.*

Leah lifted her hand. The wound was healing well, only a trace of blood was left on her skin. And the counter had suffered a definite hit from something strong enough to leave an epicenter that dented it.

She should feel fright. At the very least, a bit of anxiety. She felt neither. But she needed more. Something...concrete. Leah raced to her desk. Careened into the furniture piece, jostling papers and her stapler with her speed and inexperience at controlling it. She opened her laptop with a careful movement. Her fingers flew through the commands. She did a search.

And...

*Yes!*

The screen lit up in orange and red shades. There had been a series of massive explosions on the border between Poland and the Czech Republic. Someone in a helicopter had been on sight, taking video. She couldn't make out much through the fire, but then there was a large whoosh, and the rusted tower erupted in flames. The announcer's foreign words got louder and quicker paced, while she read the information line scrolling across the bottom of the screen. They had the camera directly on the tower as it shuddered, bent, and then toppled over.

Terrorism had been considered. Discarded for now. Authorities suspected a massive underground gas leak from an unknown source. Leah had seen enough.

She believed.

She wasn't remotely insane. Or delusional. Love was her diagnosis. She was in love! With a real man! He was real! He did exist! And it didn't matter if he was a vampire or a king, or even a pauper. Everything she'd experienced since meeting Anso had been real. His kisses. Their lovemaking. The closeness.

She was in love! And he'd said he loved her. This was euphoric. Heady. Magical.

And then it was completely deflating.

Her belly dropped as an entirely new sensation enveloped her. She recognized fear as she began shaking with it. This wasn't any fear, however. This emotion was accompanied by absolute desperation. Despair.

*Well.*

Leah had never been the type of person to sit about waiting for fate to hand her things. She went after what she wanted. She always had. She opened her laptop again. Started another search, this one with travel in mind. She needed to get to him. Book a flight back to Prague. Somehow find his castle. In a cliff somewhere in the Czech Republic. Or maybe they'd been in Slovakia.

*Crap.*

The odds were stacked against her here. She'd have to be really lucky. She didn't have much to go by. He worked for something called VAL. She started that search next.

And that's when she saw the cell phone. Placed on a shelf at her eye level along with a scrap of paper. She unfolded it with fingers that trembled.

*When you are ready, just press connect.*

# CHAPTER THIRTEEN

Akron held him back with one hand while he pulled a phone from somewhere beneath his cloak. The man had his palm against Anso's heart. He had to know how it thudded heavily with every continuing ringtone. Akron held the phone for longer than he needed, and let it ring four times before he answered. Anso lowered his jaw and settled with giving the leader of the Vampire Assassin League a baleful glare.

He tensed his muscles. Locked his teeth. His left eye twitched. He didn't make a sound, however. He was under orders.

Akron was smiling slightly as he finally answered. "Yes?"

"Oh. Thank goodness! Hi there!"

Anso's knees wavered as he heard her voice, not only through Akron's speaker, but it was audible through the door they faced, the one with a metal plate marked with numbers. Three-Eight-One. His mate was so close! He jerked involuntarily. Akron pushed against his chest. The man's hand sent Anso against the far wall, and then it held him there. Anso felt every ridge of his sword; the intricate hilt, the hammered metal that trimmed his scabbard, the blade that was jammed against his lower spine and buttocks. And then the pressure eased as his sword bit into the wall with a crunching sound.

That was going to leave damage.

Good thing it was the midst of the night, his mate lived in a secured complex, and nobody appeared to be having a fest this eve. He and Akron made quite the sight. Anso was large, but Akron topped him by a good two inches. Maybe more. The man wore his usual long, disguising black cloak. Beneath it, he'd donned black leather, distressed so it wouldn't have any shine. He wore his hood so it projected a shadow across his features. Why, if he carried a staff, he'd probably be mistaken for the Grim Reaper.

Anso was little better. They'd taken a private VAL jet. He'd washed the dirt off in the jet's shower, but he'd done it fully dressed. The only change of clothing available was menswear. Mainly suits. Sport coats. Woolen trousers, some pleated. Some not. Such attire didn't fit his image, and everything was too small in the shoulders. So, he wore his usual. Leather trousers, leather cuffs. Leather and steel neck piece. And he carried his large sword at his back. That wasn't going to go unnoticed.

If any of Leah's neighbors happened into the hall, they were in for a surprise. Leah spoke again. Anso actually kept any reaction from happening although a tremor scored his frame.

"You're the guy from the explosion, right?"

"What makes you say that?" Akron answered.

"Your voice. It's...um. Yeah. Difficult to describe. Unique."

"You are correct, Doctor Thurman. I am the man that pulled you from certain death."

"And Anso?"

"Who?" Akron asked nonchalantly.

"Oh. Please. Don't do this to me!"

Despite the lock he had on his body, Anso reacted to the pleading tone in her voice. His muscles tensed involuntarily. Akron shoved against his chest. Anso's shoulders touched the wall before the pushing stopped. The sword broke through the depth of wall with a jerk.

"Do what, my dear?"

Akron asked it with a slow, carefully modulated tone. Anso caught the growl before he got punished again. They didn't have time for this type of conversation! Sat phones were different. They could talk for as long as necessary. Cell phones were different. Calls could be traced. There was a time limit!

"I need to know where he is! Okay? Please?"

"I have a lot of associates in my firm, Doctor Thurman. I am equally fond of all of them. And well aware of what they deserve...and don't deserve."

"Please?"

"You understand he is a vampire? A real one? We do exist. Yes?"

"Yes! Yes, I do!"

Anso's head lifted. His eyes went wide. Akron winked at him. Anso flushed. Akron's smile at his blush was quick, over almost the instant it started. He cleared his throat. Spoke to Leah again.

"Are you saying you believe in us? Truly?"

"Yes! Now, please. Please? Just tell me how to find him!"

Anso pulled in a deep breath. Barely stopped the howl. But it required an act of will, and he still bit his tongue.

"You realize you sound insane."

"I don't care! I love him! I need him! I want him! Please, say you know how to find him!"

Leah sounded like she was sobbing. Anso's eyes watered, too. He didn't know what expression Akron had. He was too blurry.

"Oh, my dear. Dear. Logical Doctor Thurman...."

"Yes?"

Hope stained her voice. Anso recognized it easily. He caught a breath and then started shuddering violently. The wall behind him began dusting his shoulders and the carpet at his feet with chunks of building material.

"He is on the other side of your front door."

He heard her scream, the handle of her door wobbled. Akron released him and stepped to one side. And then Leah erupted. She launched across the hall and into his arms. And nothing had ever felt as wondrous.

She covered his face with kisses. Locked her arms about his shoulders and hugged him, and she was sobbing. And shaking. And laughing.

"Oh Anso! Anso! I love—!"

She didn't finish the declaration because he had her lips. Her perfect body. Her heart. He had everything. He lurched away from the wall, taking a section from it as his sword followed. They stumbled across the hall. Entered the dark privacy of her enclave. And from what sounded a long way away, he heard Akron's comment before Anso slammed the door shut with a foot.

"Ah. True love. It never grows old. Never."

# DEDICATION

To Martha Lester for coming up with the perfect name for my 18th vampire: Sebastian Cole. A special thank you to Joanne Dee and others who also thought of Sebastian. Thank you all!

# ABOUT THE AUTHOR

Jackie Ivie lives in the enormous state of Alaska with her husband and three very spoiled pets. She started her writing career writing hot highland historical romances for Kensington Publishing. There are now ten "Clans series" books, available in seven languages. Keeping her head in the clouds most of the time, Jackie now spends her time researching, developing, and writing her paranormal series – the Vampire Assassin League, as well as her other historical line – the Brocade Collection.

Jackie loves hearing from fans!

**www.jackieivie.com** or
**www.VampireAssassinLeague.com**

Want to keep up with the assassins of the
Vampire Assassin League?

Consider joining the Assassin Street Team at
**www.facebook.com/groups/379151425455048**